COUNTERSNATCH

Peter Wilde and Andrew Liston are invited by Cathie Hackett, who lives in the flat above, to join her and her husband for a drink that evening — but, on arrival, they learn that Cathie has been kidnapped. Puzzled by Hackett's attitude, Peter and Andrew decide to investigate. They discover where Cathie is being held, but Hackett shows no inclination to act on the information. The mystery deepens when the Hacketts' flat goes up in flames and two bodies are found in the ruins.

J. F. STRAKER

COUNTERSNATCH

Complete and Unabridged

LINFORD
Leicester

First published in Great Britain

First Linford Edition
published 2001

British Library CIP Data

Straker, J. F., (John Foster), *1904 –*
    Countersnatch.—Large print ed.—
    Linford mystery library
    1. Detective and mystery stories
    2. Large type books
    I. Title
    823.9′14 [F]

ISBN 0–7089–9747–3

Published by
F. A. Thorpe (Publishing)
Anstey, Leicestershire

Set by Words & Graphics Ltd.
Anstey, Leicestershire
Printed and bound in Great Britain by
T. J. International Ltd., Padstow, Cornwall

This book is printed on acid-free paper

1

Hamble Close, situated off Hamble Avenue, is an intrusion into Wimbledon Common: a secluded cul-de-sac of five Victorian and well detached houses, discreetly shielded from each other and from the gravelled roadway by tall, overgrown hedges that border the large and mostly unkempt gardens. The houses themselves, however, are not particularly large. Designed originally with dining and drawing and breakfast rooms on the ground floor, together with a fair-sized kitchen and scullery, they had cellars below and four bedrooms and the usual offices above. All but Number 5 have a conservatory leading from the drawing-room. But now only Numbers 1 and 5 are occupied by single families. Numbers 2 and 4 are empty and are scheduled for demolition, and Number 3, which stands at the far end of the Close, has been converted into two flats. The conversion was minimal, with the breakfast room converted into a bathroom-cum-lavatory and one of the bedrooms into a kitchen. The original front door, approached by five stone steps, serves as the entrance to both flats.

Peter Wilde shared the bottom flat with Andrew Liston, a free-lance photographer, although as a resident master at a boys' preparatory school in Hampshire it was for Peter more of a holiday retreat than a permanent residence. He had been introduced to Andrew, the sitting tenant, by his journalist brother-in-law, who had worked with Andrew in the past but was now with a north-country newspaper; and although he had moved in less than six months previously and had spent only three weeks of a Christmas vacation there he had already become attached to the place. He liked the large, high-ceilinged rooms and the quiet of the cul-de-sac. He liked it so much that he had returned for the half-term weekend to take a sickle to the long grass that had once been a lawn and to paint the conservatory. Now he was back for the four weeks of the Easter vacation, and as he turned his elderly Triumph Herald into the tree-lined avenue he was already picturing the conservatory as it might look when properly stocked and wondering where a novice should go for advice on plants. Andrew had damned the project as daft. Plants need tending, and with Peter away from the flat for two-thirds of the year who was supposed to do that? Not me, Andrew had said; I'm damned if I'll play nursemaid to a collection of pots and creepers. Peter had not been dissuaded. He was confident that once the plants were installed Andrew would come to share his enthusiasm.

A man was standing outside Number 3, bending to peer through a gap in the tall hedge. He straightened when he heard the Triumph and turned to watch it approach. Then he started to walk away, paused, and came slowly back.

Peter stopped the car and got out. 'Can I help you?' he asked.

'I'm trying to locate an old friend,' the man said.

'Oh? What name?'

3

'Warren. David Warren. I was told he lives here.'

'Here? You mean at Number 3?'

'Yes. I've rung the bell twice, but no one answers. I guess they must be out.'

Peter studied him, wondering why, if the man had reached that conclusion, he should be peering through the hedge. He was tall and robust, with a round red face and overlong brown hair. Late twenties, Peter thought.

'There's no one named Warren lives at Number 3,' he said.

'No?' The man searched his lower gum with a probing tongue. 'You sure?'

'I should be. I live here. I share the bottom flat with a friend named Liston, and the top flat is occupied by a Mr and Mrs Hackett.' Peter had yet to meet the Hacketts. They had moved in early in February, but had been away when he returned at half-term. 'You sure it was Hamble Close? Not the Avenue?'

'Ah! Could be.' The man nodded. 'Thanks. I'll try there.'

Peter watched him walk away and wondered how he had come. There was no car parked in the Close. Then he dismissed the man from his mind, collected his two suitcases from the boot, and went indoors.

The furniture in the large living-room was mostly second-hand, bought at public auctions or from junk shops, the central piece being an enormous mahogany table, oval in shape and with massive legs; the loose central leaf had warped and did not fit properly. The cushions and arms of the settee and the two club armchairs were lumpy, the covers clean but faded; the cane seats of four small upright chairs were ragged where some of the cane had broken. A gate-legged table stood in one corner of the room, a colour television set stood in another. There were neither dresser nor cupboards, but Andrew had put up numerous shelves that were crowded with books and china and sundry articles of use or interest or ornamentation. The large-patterned wallpaper had faded where the sun had caught it, the ceiling had brown circles round the two centre lights. The flooring was of oak, its only covering a couple of worn Persian-type rugs. But for Peter the blemishes detracted little from the flat's general appeal. And his bedroom furniture, which he had bought on moving in, was new and modern, with an extremely comfortable bed.

He was frying sausages and a large slice of bread when Andrew returned. Andrew stood in the kitchen doorway and flapped a hand at the blue haze.

'Bangers for tea, eh?' he said. 'Good. I'm starving. Had to skip lunch.'

'Bangers for me. Period.' Peter leaned away from the spitting fat. 'I'm hungry too, and I wasn't expecting you. What brings you back so early? Run out of film?'

'Run out of car. The bloody clutch went.' Andrew moved closer to the stove, savouring the appetising aroma. 'Eight bangers! Don't tell me you're aiming to eat the lot! You can't be that greedy.'

Peter shrugged, cut another slice of bread, and slid it into the pan. Andrew was always hungry. A giant of a man, with long arms and large feet, the most striking thing about his appearance was his hair: a fierce red in colour, it spread down in profusion from the crown of his head to obscure much of his face, culminating in a beard that he seldom bothered to trim. His eyes were blue, his teeth uneven, his nose large and flat. At present the nose was inflamed. He had a head cold.

They shared the fried bread and the sausages. 'Tell me about the Hacketts,' Peter said, pouring tea.

Andrew finished the last of the sausages. Then he leaned back in his chair and belched. The belch was deliberate. An old Chinese custom expressing appreciation, he explained to those who looked aghast at this departure from accepted behaviour. Peter suspected that what had started as a joke had become a habit.

'I told you at half-term, didn't I?' Andrew said.

'I hardly saw you at half-term. You were covering that rabies scare. All I know is that she's attractive, and considerably younger than him. What does he do, by the way?'

'For a living? So far as I know, nothing. Seems to spend most of his time following the gee-gees. And he keeps a boat somewhere down on the south coast.'

'Sail or motor?'

'I wouldn't know. But it's sea-going, so it must be fairly large.'

'And that's all he does?'

'Well, he sometimes watches the Dons when they're playing at home. And he's keen on motor racing. Seems familiar with most of the circuits.'

'Does he race himself?'

'Not now. I think he used to, in an amateurish sort of way.'

Peter sighed. 'Lucky devil! All the time and money to do as he pleases, and a smashing young wife to boot.'

'Not to boot, laddie, to bed.' Andrew helped himself to milk. He never drank tea. 'But he's certainly well-heeled. Not that he's ostentatious with it. He doesn't boast about his boat, and his Rover's at least four years old. And he's not one of your flashy dressers.'

'What's he like as a person?'

'Well, he's no extrovert. Not the expansive type. Anything I know about him, which isn't much, I've got from Cathie. She's his second wife; his first marriage ended in divorce.' Andrew shrugged. 'He's friendly enough, but I doubt if one could ever get close to him.'

'Could you get close to her?'

Andrew's bearded lips parted in a grin that was akin to a leer.

'With enthusiasm, laddie, with enthusiasm. Whenever we're down in the dark-room together — she's nuts on photography — I'm sorely tempted. Just one hint that she's available — one tiny hint, that's all — and I'd be in there grappling.' He shook his head. 'So far it hasn't happened. Too fond of her old man, I suppose.'

'Or his money.'

'Could be. Incidentally, I promised to give her a lift up to Town on Monday. There's a demonstration out Hackney way I'd planned to cover. I'll have to tell her I can't make it. No car.'

'You won't be going?'

'Probably. But by public transport.'

'I could take you,' Peter said. He had planned to visit a garden centre, but that could wait. 'I've nothing fixed for Monday.'

'Offer accepted,' Andrew said promptly. 'I take it you have no objection to Cathie Hackett as an extra passenger?'

'None whatever,' Peter said.

As they washed the dishes after the meal he told Andrew about the man he had met outside the house. Had either of the flats previously been occupied by someone named Warren? he asked. Andrew thought not. Nor, to his knowledge, was there a Warren anywhere in the Close. A Jewish family named Samuels lived in Number 1, and Number 5 was occupied by two elderly ladies, a widowed Mrs Strawan and a Miss Wellings, her sister. 'The other two houses have been empty ever since I moved in,' Andrew said. 'And that's over a year. There were squatters in Number 4 for a while. Perhaps Warren was one of them.'

'I doubt it. I got the impression he was legit.' Peter shook his head. 'You know, the more I think of it the odder it seems.'

'What does?'

'This chap I met.'

10

'Why? People are always getting addresses wrong.'

'I know. But why was he peering through the hedge? And he didn't seem at all surprised when I told him there was no one named Warren living here. It was as if he knew it already.'

'Then why would he ask?'

'I can't imagine,' Peter said. 'That's what bugs me.'

2

Cathie Hackett was tall and slim, with jet black hair framing an oval face. Watching her come down the steps, dressed in a blue suède jacket and skirt over a white polo-necked jumper and with a tight-fitting woollen cap on her head, Peter appreciated the temptation Andrew had experienced in the dark-room. Perhaps the make-up, and particularly the eye-shadow, was somewhat overdone, and he did not entirely approve of the heavy brass earrings. But he wasn't complaining. Taken as a package, Cathie Hackett was definitely a dish.

'Nice of you to give me a lift,' she said, when Andrew had introduced them. 'I get no co-operation from Ben on race days. He just clears off and leaves me to it.'

'My pleasure,' Peter said.

He felt aggrieved when Andrew ushered her into the back of the car and, festooned with cameras, took the front passenger seat for himself. He had thought to see approval in her clear grey eyes as she studied him. That had not surprised him, for although by no means vain he knew that women found him attractive. He tanned easily in the sun; easily and deep, so that the tan lasted through most of the winter, accentuating the light brown hair and the grey of his eyes and the even whiteness of his teeth. His body was hard and muscular, and at five feet eleven he looked down on most women — which was how he and they preferred it.

'Where do we drop you?' he asked.

'Would the King's Road be out of your way?'

Peter said truthfully that it would not.

She chatted as they drove. She had an appointment with her hairdresser at eleven-thirty, she said, and prior to that she was meeting Ben's cousin for coffee. He had rung that morning after Ben had left. 'He's just passing through London,' she said. 'Flying on to the States this afternoon. He was disappointed at missing Ben — apparently they've been out of touch for years — but he's prepared to make do with me.'

'I don't see how he can lose by it,' Peter said gallantly. 'Not aesthetically, anyway.'

She laughed. 'I hope we recognise each other. We've never met.' She leaned forward, so that her face was close to his. 'How about you and Andrew popping in for a drink before dinner this evening? I'd like you to meet my husband.'

'I'd like that too,' Peter said. Chanel Number Five, he thought, and liberally applied. 'All right with you, Andrew?'

'Fine,' Andrew said. 'Thanks, Cathie.'

'About six-thirty, then,' she said. 'I'm looking forward to an orgy of shopping this afternoon, but I'll be back before then. So will Ben, I hope.'

They dropped her in the King's Road. The traffic was heavy, and as Peter waited for an opportunity to pull away from the kerb Andrew suddenly sat up and leaned out of the window.

'There's Gordon Jackson! Hang on while I get a picture.'

He grabbed the camera. Recognising the familiar face, Peter waited. Then, as the traffic lights behind them changed to red and the flow dwindled, Andrew sank back into his seat.

'Okay,' he said.

He had expected an explosive situation at the demonstration, with confrontation by rival groups; but apart from some heckling and a few minor scuffles it was comparatively peaceful. 'Not worth the trip,' he said, as they lunched in a Fleet Street pub. 'Not with petrol the price it is. Gordon Jackson's worth two of that lot.'

'You can't win them all,' Peter said. 'And you're not paying for the petrol. Now, about that conservatory. Where do we go for plants?'

'Not 'we',' Andrew said. 'I'm staying. I've work to do.'

'All right, then, where do I go?'

Andrew shrugged. 'You could try Sion House, I suppose.'

'Where's that?'

'Kew — Isleworth — out that way.'

'Thanks.' Peter drained his glass. 'Well, I'm off. See you.'

He was arranging pot plants on the conservatory shelves when Andrew returned to the flat. 'What d'you think?' he asked, standing back to admire his handiwork. 'Gives the place a bit of style, eh? All that glass and emptiness was depressing.'

Andrew grunted. 'I hope you know how to look after the bloody things,' he said. 'A mass of dead foliage would be even more depressing.'

'They're mostly succulents and cacti. They don't need much tending. Or that's what the man said.'

Andrew moved round the conservatory, reading the names of the plants. 'Why not tomatoes?' he asked. 'They're colourful, aren't they? Or cucumbers, even?'

'Why not?' Peter agreed. It was typical of Andrew to think of his stomach. 'We could even grow grapes if we had some heat in the place.'

They went up to the Hacketts' flat shortly after six-thirty. There was a long wait before Andrew's ring was answered. When eventually Ben Hackett opened the door he looked surprised to see them and not, Peter thought, entirely pleased. Peter wondered if Cathie had forgotten to mention her invitation.

'Evening,' Andrew said. 'Mind if we come in?'

Taking affirmation for granted, he strode into the room. 'I'm Peter Wilde,' Peter said. 'Andrew's flat-mate.'

Hackett nodded, taking the proffered hand. Some twenty years older than his wife, whom both Andrew and Peter judged to be around twenty-seven, he was a big, solid-looking man with a florid, clean-shaven face and rough-looking skin. His hair had started to grey and showed a bald patch on the crown of his head. A well-fitting but somewhat crumpled grey suit bore witness to Andrew's assertion that he was not a flashy dresser.

'Pleased to meet you,' Hackett said. 'Come in.'

There was another man in the room. Like Hackett, he was large and solid, and although his hair showed less grey he too had a balding crown. Also clean-shaven, his complexion was paler and smoother than Hackett's. And he was several years the younger.

Hackett introduced him as Harry

Smith. As they shook hands Harry said, 'Ben and I are old friends. I'm staying with him for a few days.'

Peter drank beer, the others whisky; whisky was good for his cold, Andrew said. Peter wandered round the room while they talked. It was a large room, with a deep pile carpet on the floor and heavy velvet curtains at the windows. The furniture was modern and not much to his taste, although he suspected the armchairs were more comfortable than they looked. There was a small grand piano and a 26-inch colour television set with remote control. But it was the photographs that caught the eye. They were everywhere; hanging on the walls or standing on furniture, enlarged and expertly framed: photographs of people and places and buildings, taken in a splendid variety of localities at home and abroad. Cathie's work, Peter supposed. But the contents of an album lying on the piano were certainly not Cathie's work. They were wedding photographs, and the groom was obviously Hackett — taken at his first wedding, presumably, for he must have been at least fifteen years younger. And the bride wasn't Cathie.

'What's happened to Cathie?' Andrew asked presently. 'Isn't she back yet?'

'No,' Hackett said.

Andrew grinned. 'That'll do a power of no good to your bank balance.'

Hackett looked startled. 'How do you mean?'

'She's shopping, isn't she?'

'Shopping? Good Lord, no! Just spending a few days with her mother.' As an afterthought he added, 'In Brighton. Left this morning.'

It was the turn of Peter and Andrew to be surprised. 'Really?' Andrew said. 'Are you sure, Ben?'

'Of course I'm sure.' Hackett sounded aggrieved. With reason, Peter thought. Although Andrew had had good cause to ask the question, the girl's husband could well have considered it unwarranted. 'She fixed it last night.'

'Sorry,' Andrew said. 'I didn't mean to be nosey. It's just that Peter and I gave her a lift up to Town this morning, and she told us she had a hair appointment and intended to spend the afternoon shopping.'

'And before that she was meeting your cousin for coffee,' Peter added.

'Cousin?' Hackett said sharply. 'What cousin?'

Peter repeated what Cathie had told them. Hackett frowned and looked at Harry. 'That'd be Arthur Branch, wouldn't it?' Harry said. 'He lives in the States, doesn't he?'

'Ah, yes!' Hackett said. 'Yes, of course. Well, I wouldn't know about that. But I suppose she might have done a bit of shopping, bought her mother a present. And she'd certainly have her hair done. Her mother likes her to look nice.'

Peter was puzzled. Why should Hackett be nervous, as he undoubtedly was? His voice was strained, shrilling at times, and he kept fidgeting with his glass; twisting it in his hands, putting it down and then snatching it up to gulp at the whisky. His faint Cockney accent had become more apparent, and occasionally he dropped an aspirate. Peter noticed that most of the little finger on his left hand was missing.

"'An orgy of shopping' was how she described it.' Andrew sniffed and blew his nose. 'And she didn't mention Brighton or her mother.'

Hackett frowned. 'Any reason why she should?'

'Perhaps not. But she invited us in for a drink this evening, which is why we're here. She wouldn't have done that, would she, if she was off to Brighton?'

'She might.' Hackett poured himself another whisky. 'When you know Cathie better, Andrew, you'll find she can be bloody forgetful.' He looked at Harry. 'That's so, isn't it?'

Harry nodded and grinned, displaying yellowing teeth. 'Memory like a sieve.'

'You really believe she had forgotten she was off to Brighton when she invited us?' Andrew said, his tone incredulous.

The question was addressed to Hackett, but it was Harry who answered. 'Must have done, mustn't she?' Harry said.

'Apparently she had forgotten it even before she left the house,' Peter said. 'She didn't have any luggage. Only a handbag.'

'She didn't?' Hackett seemed non-plussed. Again he looked at Harry, to be answered with a shrug. 'I wouldn't have thought she could be that forgetful.'

'Maybe she changed her mind after you left.' Andrew suggested. 'Cancelled the visit to her mother and went shopping instead. In which case — '

'No way,' Harry interrupted. 'It's seven-thirty. She'd have been back long before now.'

'Exactly.' Andrew nodded vigorously. 'So what's keeping her? Has something happened? I mean, she could have had an accident, couldn't she? Or — well, it's a lonely walk from the bus-stop. Unless she took a taxi it's possible she — '

'Oh, come off it, man!' Harry said testily. 'Stop putting the frighteners on the poor bugger. You're giving him the shakes.' Peter realised that was true. Hackett had been uneasy before; now he was really scared. 'Look! Why don't we ring her mother, Ben? Check that she's arrived? That'll put a stop to all this nonsense.' Noting Hackett's hesitation, he said. 'Leave it to me. I'll do it.'

Hackett stared at him. 'You will?'

'Sure. No bother.'

Harry crossed to the telephone, perched himself on the arm of a convenient chair, and dialled. The receiver at his ear, he nodded at them. 'It's ringing,' he said. 'Shall I — ' He broke off and spoke into the mouthpiece. 'That you, Edie? Harry here. Harry Smith. I'm ringing from Ben's place. Staying with him for a few days.' He listened for a while. 'Yes, fine, we'll do that. But about Cathie, Edie. Has she — ' Another pause. 'Oh, she did. Good. We just wanted to check. There's been a bit of a misunderstanding this end and Ben was getting worried. Yes. Yes, I'll tell him. Do you want to speak to him? All right, then. Give Cathie my love.'

He replaced the receiver and stood up. 'She's there,' he said. 'Arrived about an hour ago. But she forgot her suitcase. Packed it last night, apparently, and then forgot to take it.' He reached for his glass. 'Well, that's Cathie for you.'

'Yes.' Obviously relieved, Hackett

picked up the whisky bottle. 'Andrew? Another beer, Peter?'

Both accepted. 'Sorry about that, Ben,' Andrew said. 'I'm not usually a pessimist. But under the circumstances — '

'Not to worry,' Hackett said. 'Forget it.'

Andrew didn't forget it. Back in their own flat he said ruefully, 'I should have kept my big mouth shut. Rabbiting on about Cathie having an accident or being raped or God knows what! If Harry hadn't thought to ring her mum Ben could have been heading for a heart attack.'

'Harry didn't,' Peter said.

'Didn't what?'

'Harry didn't ring Brighton.'

'But he did! Dammit, Peter, we saw him.'

'We saw him dial a number, but it wasn't a Brighton number. The STD code for Brighton is 0273. I know — I've got a cousin there. What's more, I'm pretty sure all the numbers have six figures. Harry only dialled six altogether, and not a seven among them.'

'How do you know that?'

'From the clicks. They were too few for a seven. I'd say none of them was higher than a four.' Peter went into the kitchen. 'How do you want your eggs? Boiled or fried?'

'Scrambled.' Andrew followed him. 'So whose number did he dial, then?'

'I suspect he just chose one at random.' Peter put butter into a saucepan. 'Make the toast, will you? I'll do the eggs. You want coffee?'

'Yes. But if — I mean — well, who was he talking to?'

'No one. The phone was dead.'

'You mean all that chat was a charade?'

'That's exactly what I mean.' Peter added milk to the melted butter and began to crack the eggs. 'For some reason or other he wanted us to believe that Cathie is in Brighton.'

'Ben too?'

'Could be. Where's the whisk?'

'Under the sink. But why would Harry pretend she's in Brighton if she isn't?'

'God knows!' Cooking utensils spilled out of the sink cupboard as Peter opened it. 'But I bet I'm right. And another thing.

How often do you suppose Harry rings Cathie's mother? Yet he dialled without bothering to look up the number.'

The toaster popped. Andrew spread butter generously on the toast.

'I suppose she *could* be in Brighton,' he said. 'We don't know for certain that she isn't.'

'Harry knows. Hence the charade. The question is, does Ben know? If he does — well, something's going on that they don't want us to know about.'

'And if Ben doesn't know?'

'Your guess is as good as mine. But I think he does. Ready with the toast?'

'Yes. Put my egg on the plate, will you? I don't like it on the toast. Makes it soggy.'

They discussed the matter further as they ate. Although admitting the strength of Peter's argument, Andrew was still sceptical of his conclusion. It was too way-out, it didn't make sense. For instance, wasn't it possible that Harry, believing Ben's statement that Cathie had gone to Brighton and impatient to end the argument, had pretended to telephone rather than go through the rigmarole of looking up the number and perhaps involving himself in a long telephonic conversation? Couldn't that explain why he had chosen to ring rather than leave it to Ben? Remembering how often he had arrived at wrong conclusions before, when murder had dislocated the Autumn term, Peter admitted that it was certainly possible. But he did not believe it. He was convinced he was right.

'However, it's none of our business,' he said, taking the empty dishes to the sink. 'If they like to make mysteries, let them. Come and inspect the conservatory.'

'It's only a few hours since the last inspection,' Andrew said. 'They won't have grown much, will they? Still, if you insist — '

Examining the plants again, reading the names aloud — acacias, freesias, pelargoniums, begonias — Peter wondered idly how long his new-found interest in horticulture would last. It would probably depend on the degree of success he managed to achieve. 'I don't know why they have to give these things such impossible names,' he said. 'Still, most of them have — well, nicknames, I suppose you'd call them. That's a rat's tail, and that's a prickly pear. And that chap there is an Easter cactus. The nurseryman suggested we put it in a hanging basket. Most of them can go outside during the summer, he said, but I don't remember which. I'll have to look it up.'

'Must have cost a packet,' Andrew said.

'They weren't cheap,' Peter admitted.

'Well, don't forget the tomatoes,' Andrew said. 'Not if you expect help from me. A Cathie style memory will get you nowhere.'

'I won't forget.' Peter frowned. 'Although I don't believe Cathie is as forgetful as those two make out.'

'Ah! We're back to that, are we?' Andrew led the way into the sitting-room. 'Well, neither do I.'

'I suppose it's just possible she could have forgotten to take her suitcase,' Peter said. 'But it's inconceivable that when she invited us for drinks she could have

28

forgotten, even temporarily, that she was on her way to Brighton.'

Andrew nodded. 'From which you argue, of course, that she wasn't.' He sat down and started to fill his pipe. He took his time over lighting it. When eventually the tobacco was burning to his satisfaction he said thoughtfully, 'Know what I'd like to do?'

'What?'

'Ring her mother. Check for ourselves. Unethical, of course; as you said, it's none of our business. But that's what I'd like.'

'So would I. However, ethics apart, we couldn't. We don't know her mother's name and we don't know the number. And we could hardly ask Ben.'

'I know her name. It's Belsham.'

'How do you know that?'

'Cathie was an actress before she married Ben. Nothing big, mind you. Bit parts, TV adverts, that sort of thing. She showed me her Press cuttings once, and some of them gave her name. Cathie Belsham.'

Peter was intrigued. Andrew was right, of course, they had no business to interfere. And yet . . .

'Belsham's an uncommon name,' he said. 'I wonder how many there are in Brighton?'

'I could check with Directory Enquiries.'

'Yes. Why not?'

Andrew checked. 'Well, at least we've got her located,' he said. 'There's only the one.'

'Really? Did they tell you the number?'

'Yes.'

Peter hesitated, but not for long. Curiosity was stronger than scruples.

'Try it, Andrew. Don't give your name. Just ask for Cathie, and hang up if she's there.'

'You think we should?'

'No. But we're going to, aren't we?'

Andrew dialled without further comment. Peter heard him ask for Cathie. Andrew listened for a few moments and then hung up.

'A man answered,' he said. 'He says he's never heard of Cathie Hackett.'

3

They sat drinking and talking into the small hours of the Tuesday morning. Andrew's telephone call had established that Cathie was not with her mother in Brighton, that Mrs Belsham did not even live there; and since Hackett must certainly be aware of that latter fact it followed that he must also be aware of the former and had known that Harry's telephone call was a hoax. So why had he not shown proper concern at Cathie's continued absence? The answer seemed to be that he knew where she was and what she was doing, and that neither danger nor distress threatened her. But if that were the case, why should he and Harry have been at such pains to conceal the truth? Was the truth unpleasant — detrimental — embarrassing? Embarrassing, Andrew thought. Cathie had left Ben for another and probably younger man and Ben could not bring himself to admit it. He had told Harry because Harry was an old and close friend, but he was telling no one else. Then why had Cathie not taken a suitcase, Peter objected, and why had she invited them for drinks that evening? And where did Ben's cousin fit in? Maybe he didn't, Andrew said after much thought. Maybe Cathie had invented him for their benefit, although it was difficult to see why. Or perhaps Ben's cousin *was* the other man. Anyway, she had gone to meet her lover, whoever he might be, and she hadn't taken a suitcase because it was not until after they met that she finally decided to go away with him. Just like that? Peter said. Wouldn't she first have returned to the flat for her things? Maybe there wasn't time, Andrew suggested, maybe he really did have a plane to catch. Or maybe she feared Ben might return while she was there, and couldn't bring herself to face him.

Peter still had objections, but he agreed that Andrew was probably not far from the truth of it. And that posed a further problem. As the days passed and Cathie failed to return, how would Hackett explain her absence? He would inevitably become involved in further deceit, in more and more improbable lies, so that the situation would become increasingly more difficult and more embarrassing for all three of them. Would it not be made easier, for him as well as for them, if he were told that they had realised the truth; not that Cathie had left him, but that she was not with her mother in Brighton? They need not mention that they had tried to contact Mrs Belsham, since that would invite resentment, even anger. They could say merely that they knew, from listening to the number Harry had dialled, that he could not have been talking to someone in Brighton, and leave it at that. If Hackett decided to explain the reason for the deceit, well and good. If he chose not to, then at least he would not be forced to maintain what could become an untenable position.

They tackled him after breakfast. Both Hackett and Harry were unshaven and still in pyjamas; but whereas Harry lounged in a chair looking comfortably replete, a full cup of coffee in his hand and the greasy remains of bacon and egg on his plate, Hackett looked even more drawn than on the previous evening. There was no bacon and egg for him, merely an unfinished slice of buttered toast. If he had slept at all, Peter decided, it had been an uneasy sleep.

'Bit early to come calling, isn't it?' Harry said.

'I know,' Andrew said. 'And I'm sorry. But we wanted to catch Ben before he went out.'

'Are you going out, Ben?' Harry asked.

Hackett shook his head. 'What's up, Andrew?' he asked.

Without preamble, Andrew told him. 'We weren't intending to snoop,' he explained, noting the frown on Hackett's face. 'But Peter happens to know the Brighton code, and listening to the clicks he realised that Harry hadn't dialled it.'

'Clever of him,' Harry said.

'It seemed kindest to tell you, Ben,' Peter said. 'Otherwise it could have been embarrassing for all of us. But we're not asking for an explanation. It's your affair, nothing to do with us. We just thought you ought to know.'

Hackett sat down and looked at Harry. There was a long silence. Then Harry said, 'Want me to tell them, Ben?'

'If you like.'

Harry put down his coffee. 'Cathie's been snatched,' he said. 'Kidnapped.'

They were shocked into exclamations of concern. 'Christ, Ben, but I'm sorry,' Andrew said. 'We never imagined anything like that.'

Hackett shrugged. 'You thought she'd left me, I suppose.'

'Well, we — ' Andrew stopped. It would be cruel to admit it. 'They've contacted you already, have they?'

'They telephoned yesterday afternoon,' Harry said. 'That's why I'm here. Ben rang me, and naturally I came right over. They're holding her to ransom.'

'How much?' Peter asked.

'A hell of a lot,' Harry said. 'And he has until the end of the week to raise it. Otherwise' — He shrugged. 'Well, you know the form.'

'Have you contacted the police?' Peter asked.

Hackett shook his head. 'They warned me not to.'

'They always do,' Andrew said. 'I've covered a few kidnappings, and I've never known it otherwise.'

'They also warned him not to confide in anyone,' Harry said. 'It might reach the Law second-hand. Hence the 'Gone to Mother' story.'

Peter thought that last remark unnecessarily facetious. He began to dislike Harry. 'It won't reach the police through us,' he said. 'Although I think you're wrong not to tell them, Ben. Paying the ransom doesn't always ensure the victim's safety. You must know that.'

'Peter's right,' Andrew said. 'Tell them, Ben. It's the safest course.'

Ben shook his head. 'I can't risk it, Andrew. I'll have to try and raise the money.'

'You'll manage it,' Harry said. He sounded almost cheerful. 'You know you will. And if you find yourself short of a few quid — well, what are friends for, eh?'

Ben said nothing. 'I'm afraid neither Peter nor I can offer that sort of help,' Andrew said. 'But if there's anything else we can do you've only to name it.'

'Thanks,' Ben said. 'But there's nothing, I'm afraid.'

'Don't be too sure. Peter here is by way of being a bit of a sleuth. Term before last there was a rash of murders at his school and he solved the lot. Who knows? He might be able to do something for you.'

'Andrew's exaggerating,' Peter said hastily. 'I'm no sleuth, the police solved it long before I did. But there was a chap snooping around the house when I arrived Saturday afternoon. Could he be mixed up in this? He said he was looking for someone named Warren and had been given this address.'

Ben shook his head and looked at Harry. Harry shrugged. 'Could be, I suppose,' he said. 'What did he look like?'

Peter's description failed to elicit recognition, and after further expressions of sympathy and support he and Andrew left. 'Why the hell did you try to get me involved, dammit?' Peter said irritably as they descended the stairs. 'I don't want it, I couldn't do it, and anyway it's none of my business.'

Andrew grinned. 'Law and order is everyone's business. And you've damn all else to do. You can't fiddle with those bloody plants all day.'

'And where would you suggest I start?'

'You're the sleuth, laddie, not me. Although you might try the hairdresser's, I suppose. Still, suit yourself. Now — can you run me up to Town or do I go public?'

'I'll take you.'

'Thanks.' Andrew went into the kitchen to brew coffee. 'Poor old Ben! What did you make of Harry?'

'Well, he's obviously a good friend to Ben. But I can't say I liked him. Too offhand, I thought.'

In the half hour that elapsed before leaving the flat Peter reflected on Andrew's suggestion that he should interest himself in the kidnapping and began to find merit in it. It had a certain appeal. As Andrew had said, he had nothing in particular to do, and his experience the previous November had given him a taste for detection. True, he had made mistakes in his self-imposed investigation. But at least he had unearthed facts which, even if all were not directly connected with the case in hand, were at least on the fringe of it. Even the police, he suspected, had been unaware of some of them. He had not been entirely unsuccessful.

He would have a go, he told Andrew, provided the latter was prepared to help — a condition which Andrew cheerfully accepted. 'You're on,' he said. 'Watson to your Holmes, eh?'

Peter drove him to Victoria and returned to Chelsea. They had dropped Cathie in the King's Road, and although there was no certainty that that was where her hairdresser was located it was the only lead he had. Hackett would know, of course. But to ask Hackett would be to reveal his intention and that, he had decided, just wasn't on. Hackett would probably disapprove of what he would see as unauthorised meddling. So why arouse his ire when, as seemed ninety-nine per cent certain, the meddling would come to nothing?

In fact, it came to a little more than nothing. Yes, the receptionist told him at the second salon he visited, Mrs Hackett was one of their customers. Success stopped there. No, she said, after consulting the register, Mrs Hackett had not kept the appointment, nor had she telephoned to cancel it. Disappointed, Peter returned to the car. Unable to find a free meter he had taken a chance and had parked on a yellow line. But chance wasn't with him that morning. A policeman was awaiting his return.

'Sorry, Officer,' Peter said. 'But I can't have been more than a few minutes. Just popped across the road to the hair-dresser.'

'A haircut takes more than a few minutes, sir,' the officer said.

'Oh, I wasn't having my hair cut. It was a ladies' salon.' Seeking to impress, he added, 'I'm trying to trace a missing person. The wife of a friend.'

'Is that so?' The man seemed unimpressed. 'Well, anyway, sir, your car is parked on a yellow line and is obstructing the traffic. May I see your driving licence and insurance certificate, please?'

Peter had left his insurance certificate at the flat and was told to take it to his local police station within three days. 'At the same time you might care to tell them about your friend's wife,' the policeman said. 'That's the proper place to inquire after a missing person.'

'I might do that,' Peter said. 'Does this mean a summons?'

'Very probably,' the constable said.

Peter took the certificate to the police station that afternoon. The desk sergeant was friendly, and with the official business concluded they chatted for a while. It was partly the friendliness and partly the beat constable's suggestion that prompted Peter to seek professional advice on the task he had undertaken. Kidnapping had become all too common. Although individual circumstances would vary, the police must surely have a set procedure common to most.

'May I ask you a question, Sergeant? How does one set about finding someone who has been kidnapped?'

'Eh?' The sergeant's brow creased in a frown. 'Is that a serious question, sir? Has someone actually been kidnapped?'

'Good Lord, no!' The police now had his name and address, they might decide to investigate. 'Just curious, that's all.' The explanation sounded weak. He attempted to embroider it. 'I'm a writer, you see.'

'Ah!' The sergeant looked relieved. 'Well, they say truth is stranger than fiction, but there's a lot happens in books that wouldn't happen in real life. Too many coincidences, for a start. Would it be a thriller you're writing?'

'Sort of.'

'About a kidnapping?'

'Yes.'

'There's only two solutions to that, Mr Wilde. Pay up or inform the police. Preferably the latter.'

'No alternatives? Nothing a private eye could do?'

'Not in real life,' the sergeant said. 'In a book — well, that's different, I suppose. Like someone sees the car and notes the number, or gets curious about mysterious comings and goings at the hide-out. Know what I mean? And then there's photographs. Ever see a film called 'Blow Up'?'

Peter nodded. He realised that this was getting him nowhere, but having started the charade he had to go along with it.

'It was on TV,' he said.

'Yes. Well, remember how this young fellow was taking photographs in a park, and when he blew them up later he saw where a body had been hidden in the bushes? You could use something like that, couldn't you?' The sergeant frowned. 'Wilde, eh? I don't know as I've read any of your books.'

Peter resisted the temptation to say that his pen name was John Creasey. 'Few people have,' he said.

He considered the sergeant's 'coincidences' as he drove back to the flat. There would certainly have to be a car; but since he had no idea where Cathie had been snatched he had nowhere to look for witnesses. It couldn't have happened in the King's Road. Forcibly to kidnap a girl in a busy London street would cause too much commotion, the police would be almost instantly involved; and if the kidnapping had been accomplished by trickery no one would have noticed. As for photographs . . .

Photographs! How many had Andrew taken of Gordon Jackson? Two? Three? It was possible that Cathie had arranged to meet the man claiming to be Ben's cousin where they had dropped her near the hairdresser, in which case the man could have been caught by Andrew's camera. If he were genuine, then even if some years had elapsed since Hackett had seen his cousin he should be able to recognise him; although what sort of a lead that might provide, with the cousin back in the States, was problematical. On the other hand, if the man was an impostor and therefore presumably the kidnapper, unless he and Cathie appeared together in a photograph there would be no way of identifying him and no lead at all.

Andrew was equally pessimistic, but he produced copies of the photographs, two in number. In each there was a background of people of both sexes, but Cathie was not among them. 'That doesn't mean the so-called cousin is not in the pictures,' Peter said hopefully. 'I vote we show them to Ben, just in case.'

'Wouldn't the two of them be together?' Andrew said. 'They should have had time to meet before those pictures were taken.'

'Not necessarily. They were strangers, remember, they wouldn't just rush into each other's arms.'

Sipping beer, Peter studied the photographs again. But it was not until he put down the one he was holding that he saw what his thumb had hidden.

'Andrew, look!' he exclaimed. 'That chap on the extreme right, the one with the briefcase. Notice anything?'

Andrew looked. 'Such as what?'

'Immediately to his left, on the edge of the picture, there's what looks like someone's arm. In blue.'

Andrew peered closer. 'So?'

'Cathie was wearing a blue suède jacket,' Peter said. 'Remember? It could be her. In which case the chap with the briefcase is probably the man she was meeting.'

Andrew found a magnifying glass. 'Well, Cathie or not, the person in blue has his or her back to the camera,' he said. 'It's the elbow you can see. Which suggests the two were not together. They're moving in opposite directions.'

'All the same, I vote we show it to Ben. Only don't let on we're working on it.'

Ben and Harry were drinking whisky. The television set was switched on, but only Harry was watching. Ben looked terrible. There were dark circles under his eyes, and when he spoke his voice was slurred. Yet oddly enough he managed at the same time to appear less nervous. Peter had the impression that somewhere down the dark tunnel he was seeing a glimmer of light.

Or was it the drink working in him?

'No,' Ben said, when Peter showed him the photograph and pointed out the man with the briefcase. 'Don't know him.'

'He's not your cousin?'

'Cousin? What cousin?'

'The one from the States. What's his name? Alfred, is it?'

Ben shook his head. 'Not him.'

'Do you recognise any of the others?'

Ben gave the photograph a cursory glance. 'No. No one.'

'Let me see,' Harry said.

He studied the photograph more carefully than Ben had done. 'Sorry,' he said eventually. 'They're all strangers to me.' He got up and switched off the television. 'Now, how about a drink? Ben's not quite himself this morning or I'm sure he'd have asked you.'

Both Peter and Andrew declined. 'Have you and Ben been friends for long?' Andrew asked.

'Ten — twelve years. Something like that. Why?'

'No reason,' Andrew said. 'Just curiosity.'

Peter too was curious. Although he had referred to Ben's cousin as Alfred, moments later he had remembered that, according to Harry the previous evening, the name should have been Arthur. Yet neither Ben nor Harry had corrected him. Why?

He was reading in bed when Andrew came into his room carrying a glass of hot milk. His scarlet pyjamas clashed horribly with his hair and beard.

'Did you know the Hacketts lived in Ipswich before they moved here in February?' Andrew asked.

'No. What of it?'

Andrew seated himself on the bed and sipped. 'You did say you didn't want any milk?'

'Yes. What about Ipswich?'

'It's Cathie's home town, and Ben had been living there for some time when they met.' Andrew frowned. 'That's odd! What's her mother doing in Brighton?'

'She isn't. Remember? Anyway, people move.' Peter put down the book. 'What are you getting at, Andrew? I presume you're getting at something.'

'Well, if the cousin hasn't been in touch with Ben for years, how did he know Ben's telephone number? It's not in the book yet.'

'Directory Enquiries, I suppose.'

'That's where you're wrong, laddie,' Andrew said, with an air of infantile triumph. 'Because if he didn't know Ben had moved he'd be looking for an Ipswich number, not a London one.'

4

They tried to sort fact from fiction over breakfast the following morning. Cousin or not, that the man who had telephoned Cathie had known Hackett's number seemed to give the lie to his statement that he was merely passing through London and had not been in touch with Ben for years. 'And that puts him among the kidnappers,' Peter said. 'No reason to lie if he were genuine.'

'True.' Andrew buttered his third slice of toast and reached for the marmalade. 'Personally, I doubt if Arthur Branch exists.'

'So do I. Though God knows why they should pretend he does. Why not say straight out that there's no cousin and that therefore the man's a phoney?'

Andrew nodded. He was a messy as well as a voracious eater. There were crumbs in his beard and on the tablecloth around his plate, there was marmalade on the butter where he had used his own knife instead of the butter knife. His cup sat in its saucer in a pool of coffee, which had slopped over the rim of the cup whenever he rested an elbow on the warped centre leaf of the table. There were usually food stains down the front of his pullover or on the lapels of his jacket, and the speed at which he devoured his food often led to hiccups. Watching him dig into the marmalade jar with his knife Peter wondered, as he had wondered before, why he did not feel disgust at his friend's uncouth table manners. And he didn't. Somehow with Andrew they failed to matter.

Andrew sneezed and helped himself to coffee. 'It beats me why they should have picked on Cathie,' he said. 'Ben may be wealthy, but you'd never guess it from his appearance or his life-style. He doesn't live in a bloody great mansion, he doesn't drive around in a Rolls, he doesn't entertain lavishly. True, he doesn't work for a living, so presumably he has private means. But apart from his boat — and for all anyone knows he could be buying that on H.P. — there's absolutely nothing to indicate to an outsider that he's loaded.' He gulped down the coffee, leaned back, patted his stomach — which, considering his appetite, was reasonably flat — and belched. 'So why Cathie? I'd say it's because the kidnappers have someone on the inside, someone who could make a reasonable estimate of what Ben is worth. Not necessarily a close friend, but certainly an acquaintance.'

'One of his contacts in the racing world, perhaps,' Peter suggested.

'Could be.' Andrew stood up, selected an apple, rubbed it on his sleeve and bit into it. 'And if he happens to have visited the flat I may have seen him. Anyway, I'm going to blow up those shots of Gordon Jackson and see if I can recognise any of the men in the background. I know Ben and Harry said they couldn't, but I reckon we can ignore that.'

While Andrew was in the cellar, where his darkroom and photographic equipment were housed, Peter washed up and hoovered the room and fussed over his plants. He was still fussing over them when Andrew returned with the enlargements and threw them on the table.

'Nothing,' Andrew said. 'Absolutely damn all.'

Background faces that had been almost indistinguishable in the original photographs were clearer now, and Peter studied them carefully. Almost immediately he saw a face he recognised. It was partially obscured by another, but there was no doubt in his mind. This was a face he had seen before.

His exclamation of triumph brought Andrew to peer over his shoulder. 'Recognise someone?'

'Yes.' Peter pointed to the face. 'Look! Know who that is? If I'm not very much mistaken he was best man at Ben's first wedding.'

'How the hell do you know that?'

'Monday evening, while you were rabbiting with Ben and Harry, I had a look at some of the photographs. I've never seen such a collection. They're all over, aren't they?'

'I told you, Cathie's nuts on photography.'

'She must be. Anyway, there was an album on the piano that isn't Cathie's work, and it contained a picture of a wedding group. Ben was obviously the groom, but it must have been taken at his first wedding, for he looked a lot younger. I don't remember what the bride looked like — she was on his left — but this fellow' — Peter stabbed the face with a finger — 'He was on Ben's right. The best man, presumably.'

'You're sure?'

'Positive. Look! The left side of his face is disfigured by an enormous birthmark. And the best man's was the same.'

So they knew the face of the kidnapper. But how to put a name to the face? Ben could do so, no doubt. In fact, if his scrutiny of the photograph had been closer than they had supposed he might already have done so. But whatever Ben knew he obviously wasn't telling. And Peter had no intention of asking. Yet without a name further progress was impossible. And although originally he had been reluctant to undertake the investigation, now that he had become involved he was determined to press ahead.

'Okay,' he said, after due consideration. 'We'll pay them another visit. It's only neighbourly to ask if there's been any further development. You keep them talking, and I'll take a second look at that wedding photograph. It was a professional job, so the photographer's name and address should be on the back. Maybe we can get a lead from him.'

'If he's still in business.' Andrew frowned. 'What do I talk about? The weather? The industrial situation? The Cup Final? You tell me, eh?'

Peter found that difficult. On their previous visits upstairs their welcome had been polite but far from warm. Their absence was clearly preferable to their presence, and yet another visit, with no clear purpose to it, would probably be resented. Nor could the visit be confined to a brief inquiry into possible further developments, to which the answer would undoubtedly be 'none'. To make a beeline for the album would look suspicious, he must appear to inspect it out of idle curiosity rather than from intent. And that would take time.

'You have a point,' he admitted. 'I mustn't be involved in the conversation, so it has to be a topic that doesn't concern me. Tell you what. So far the Press hasn't got wind of the kidnapping, and that's how Ben wants it. Why not put forward the view that publicity could be helpful? Offer to arrange it? They'll veto the suggestion, but never mind that. Just keep talking; hold their attention while I do my stuff. I'll be as quick as I can, but I mustn't make it look too obvious.'

As Peter had anticipated, their reception was cool. No, Harry said, assuming the office of spokesman, there had been no further contact with the kidnapper and none was expected before the end of the week, when the time limit for payment of the ransom expired. Also as anticipated, when Andrew raised the issue of publicity it was immediately rejected. Ignoring their growing hostility, Andrew pressed doggedly on with his argument. Only when he saw Peter move away from the piano did he desist.

'That was bloody embarrassing,' he said, when they were once more downstairs. 'They obviously thought I had an axe to grind, that I was out to make money by selling the story.' He headed for the kitchen. 'I need a beer. Did you get the photographer's address?'

'I got it. It's in Lewisham.'

'Lewisham, eh?' Andrew took a can from the refrigerator, poured expertly, and drank deep. Exhaling, he sucked the froth from his moustache. 'So that's our destination for this afternoon, is it?'

'Not this afternoon,' Peter said. 'Now.'

'What, before lunch?'

'Why not? We can get something to eat down there.'

The photographer's studio was still at the same address and under the same name, and the proprietor, a Mr Eastgate, looked as if he had already been old when the wedding photograph was taken. Peter explained their mission. They were making inquiries on behalf of a firm of solicitors in New Zealand, he said (New Zealand had seemed sufficiently distant to deter anyone from checking by telephone) who were trying to trace a possible beneficiary under a will. Their information was meagre, he said, but a photograph taken at a wedding in the Lewisham area (Lewisham had seemed a reasonably safe bet) some time in the mid-sixties showed the man in question with the bride and groom, apparently as best man. 'We don't know his name and there is no information on the bride,' he said, 'but the groom was a man named Hackett.'

'And we took the photographs?' Mr Eastgate said.

'Yes.'

Mr Eastgate frowned. 'We keep records, of course, but they wouldn't contain the best man's name.'

'But you'd have the date of the wedding, wouldn't you, and other details?'

'Yes.' He hesitated. 'Hackett, you say?'

'Yes.'

'You wouldn't know the serial number of the photograph?'

'Yes,' Peter said. 'One-one-six-four-stroke-seven.'

'Ah!' Mr Eastgate brightened. 'That makes it easier.'

Peter hoped it would. The date would enable them to consult the files of the local newspaper, which might well contain a report on the wedding. And presumably church and registry office records were available for inspection. Didn't the best man usually sign the register?

The frown was back on Mr Eastgate's face when he returned. 'Are you sure you have the correct serial number, sir?' he asked.

'Why?' Peter said. 'Can't you find it?'

'Oh, yes. It's one of a set of photographs we took at a wedding in Saint Patrick's on the second of May 1964.'

'Then what's the problem?'

'The bridegroom's name wasn't Hackett,' the photographer said. 'Nothing like it. It was Fillol.'

5

'So he changed his name,' Andrew said as they returned to the car to consider their next move. Saint Patrick's was out. According to Mr Eastgate it had been completely gutted by fire and was in the process of being rebuilt. 'I wonder why.'

'Could be connected with his change of fortune,' Peter said.

'How do you mean?'

'There were no tails or toppers in that wedding photograph. He wasn't rich then. Did someone leave him a packet on the condition that he changed his name to Hackett? It happens.'

'Could be.' Frowning, Andrew tugged at his beard. 'You know, Fillol's an unusual name, but I'm sure I've come across it before. Can't think where, though.'

'Wasn't there a pro tennis player named Fillol?'

'Was there? I wouldn't know. Tennis

isn't my scene. Anyway, what now?'

'Well, if he was married here he could have been living in the district. Why don't we check with the phone book? If there are any Fillols listed they are almost certain to be relatives. As you say, it's an unusual name.'

'It might go further than that,' Andrew said. 'The fellow who telephoned Cathie claimed to be Ben's cousin. Well, maybe he is. I mean, why pretend to be a cousin? Why not just a friend? So if we find a Fillol it could be we've found the kidnapper.'

'We should be so lucky!' Peter started the engine. 'But it's certainly an encouraging thought.'

There was only one Fillol in the district listed in the telephone directory: D. S. Fillol, 57 Witney Lane, S.E.6. Witney Lane proved to be a long straight road leading slightly uphill from Rushey Green, with small villas tightly packed on either side, their tiny front gardens enclosed by low brick walls. Number 57 was distinguished from its neighbours by a monkey-puzzle tree, and

Peter welcomed the tree as an unexpected bonus. They wanted to watch Number 57 without attracting the occupants' attention, and with the other houses almost identical the tree would enable them to identify the house from a distance. He parked the Herald between two other cars on the opposite side of the road and some thirty yards away, and cut the engine. Before deciding on further action he wanted a glimpse of some of the people who occupied or visited Number 57.

'What's the big idea?' Andrew protested. 'Why park? I thought we were just going to locate the place and then find somewhere to eat. Come back after lunch.' He looked at his watch. 'Dammit, Peter, it's well after one! No wonder my stomach's rumbling.'

'It's always rumbling,' Peter said. 'Damned thing never stops. All right, go and eat. There's a pub at the bottom of the road.' As an afterthought he added, 'And bring me back a sandwich.'

Left to himself, Peter sat and watched the house and wondered why he was there. He hardly knew Hackett, he didn't particularly like him, and he had met his wife just the once. So why was he involving himself so thoroughly in the man's affairs? Hackett hadn't requested his help, by his lies and evasions he had plainly rejected it. So where was the motivation? A genuine sympathy for another's anguish? A proper regard for the law, a personal protest against the illegal use of force? A touch of the Sir Galahads? Peter would have liked to think it was a mixture of some or all of these, but deep down he knew it wasn't. He was there out of curiosity, his motive was almost entirely selfish. This was an adventure, it was intriguing, it was exciting. It even hinted at danger; not too much, but enough to add spice. Above all it presented a challenge to the flair for detection he had thought to discover in himself the previous autumn term.

He was watching Andrew return up the road when a woman came out from Number 57. The binoculars were in his lap and he managed a brief glimpse of her profile as she went through the gate. Then she turned and walked away down the hill, and he put down the binoculars and waited for Andrew. Andrew had not known that the woman had come from Number 57, but from habit he had looked at her. Fortyish, he thought, perhaps under rather than over. A small rather stringy looking woman with auburn hair, probably dyed — it had that dry look — and a long thin face. 'Not badly dressed,' he added. 'But fussy. Know what I mean?'

Peter nodded. 'You really notice them, don't you? What's in the sandwiches?'

'Ham in that lot, cheese and pickles in the other. They're a bit mean with the butter, but the bread's fresh. Plastic, but fresh.'

'I'll try the ham. But first I'm going to move the car. We're on the wrong side of the house. Practically everyone goes down the road when they leave, not up. The shops, I suppose.'

He moved the car and ate the sandwiches. Andrew closed his eyes and lay back. Cars and pedestrians moved up and down the road, and some of the

returning pedestrians eyed them curiously, no doubt having noticed them
before and wondering why they were still
there. At a quarter to three the woman
who had left Number 57 earlier returned.
Peter gave Andrew a nudge with his
elbow and watched as she inserted a key
in the lock and disappeared inside. He
decided that Andrew's description of her
had been remarkably accurate.

Andrew stretched and yawned. 'If she's
been shopping she hasn't bought much,'
he said. 'Nothing that wouldn't go in her
handbag. Anyway, it's early closing.
What's the time?'

'Two-fifty.'

'Really? How long do we keep this up,
Peter?'

If D. S. Fillol had to work for a living,
Peter said, he might come home for
lunch, but he certainly wouldn't be
popping in and out of the house during
the afternoon; and as he hadn't come
home for lunch he was unlikely to return
before knocking off for the day. That
wouldn't be before five o'clock and could
be later. 'Take a walk if you're bored,' he

said. 'Go window shopping. I'm staying put.'

Andrew sighed and settled down again. Exercise, he said, had never been his strong suit. But by five-fifteen he was getting restless. Over four bloody hours they had sat there, he protested, and to what end? Maybe D. S. Fillol worked at home, maybe he didn't work at all. Maybe he was on holiday. He could even be dead. 'Why don't we ring the damned bell and ask to see him? Let's have some action, Peter. I'm not just bored, I'm bloody moribund.'

Peter refused to be pressured. Ringing the bell could defeat the object of their vigil, which was to see without being seen. 'We'll give it another half hour,' he said. 'If nothing breaks by then we'll go home. Okay?'

'Do I have a choice?' Andrew blew his nose loudly. 'Any sandwiches left?'

'A couple of cheese and pickles.'

Peter listened to him munching and willed for something to break, but the half hour passed without incident. Andrew wasn't watching the clock and Peter waited another ten minutes. Then he slapped Andrew on the knee and started the engine.

'That's it,' he said. 'We're off.'

He had put the car into gear and was about to pull out from the kerb when a man who had come up the hill from behind stepped off the pavement in front of the Herald and started to cross the road; then, realising that the engine was running, he stopped and looked at them. Peter waved him on, and the man raised a hand in acknowledgement. Only then did Peter notice the large birthmark that disfigured the left side of his face.

He cut the engine. 'Andrew, look!' he said in a near whisper. 'That's him!'

Andrew looked. 'D. S. Fillol?'

'I don't know, do I? But it's definitely the man in the photograph.'

The man reached the opposite pavement, walked a few paces to where a white Morris Traveller was parked, unlocked the rear of the car and removed a case, and relocked it. For a moment he paused, staring down the hill. Then he pushed open the gate of Number 57 and went in.

'Well, well, well!' Andrew said, boredom gone. 'So now we have him. Question is, what do we do with him?'

'That's the sixty-four dollar question,' Peter said.

'Then I move we discuss it over a pie and a pint in the nearest hostelry. I'm bloody starving. Not to mention thirsty.'

'You surprise me,' Peter said.

He made a note of the Traveller's number before restarting the engine.

They were on their second pie and pint at the Red Squirrel, the nearest pub, when Andrew said, 'I suppose D. S. Fillol really is our man? I find it difficult to comprehend how anyone could kidnap his cousin's wife and hold her to ransom. Very unnatural.'

'I don't,' Peter said. 'There was a similar case some years back, when a man kidnapped his niece. Kilburn, I think it was. No, what I find difficult to accept is that Cathie is being held captive in that house. I mean — well, a small suburban semi as the headquarters of a bunch of villains! It seems so incongruous.'

'They could be holding her elsewhere.' Andrew drained his glass and belched. 'I don't know about you, Peter, but I could manage another of those. Real ale is rare these days. One ought to make the most of it.'

'You get them,' Peter said. 'It's your round. I need the loo. Only make mine a Scotch.'

'Philistine!' Andrew said.

He was still at the bar when Peter returned. 'Don't look now,' he said, 'but guess who's just come in.'

'D. S. Fillol?' Peter said hopefully.

'No, the woman. And she's chosen to sit at the table next to ours.'

6

Andrew had described her as a 'fussy dresser'. Peter was inclined to agree. She wore a green trouser suit over a frilly white blouse, the blouse fastened at the neck by an enormous cameo brooch. Several thin gold chains were draped around her neck, and when she lifted her glass he saw that her fingers were heavily adorned with rings and that there were bangles round her wrist. Her face was sharply sculptured, with high cheek bones. Peter thought it had a sour look, as if life had been hard and was likely to get harder.

'Mrs D. S. Fillol, eh?' Andrew said.

'I imagine so.'

'Do we chat her up?'

'We can try. Although if she's involved in the kidnapping she'll not give anything away. Looks a bit of a sourpuss, too. What's she drinking?'

'Vodka. 'The usual, please, Ed,' she told

the barman. It turned out to be vodka and tonic with a dash of lime.

'A regular, eh?' Peter picked up his glass. 'Well, smile nicely when you sit down and hope for some sort of response.'

They smiled nicely. Rather unexpectedly the woman smiled back, and the smile seemed to light up her face. It was a cheerful, friendly smile, faintly provocative. Encouraged, Peter said, 'Not very crowded, is it?'

'Not very,' the woman agreed. 'But then it's early. And it's usually slack on a Wednesday, I don't know why.' She had a pleasant voice with just the hint of an accent. Peter decided she could be Irish. 'Do you live in these parts? I haven't seen you in here before, have I?'

'No to both questions,' Peter said. 'This your local, is it?'

'You might say that.'

'The beer's good,' Andrew said. 'Real ale.'

'Is it?' She smiled. 'I wouldn't know. I don't drink beer. I prefer vodka.'

She illustrated her preference by

draining her glass. 'Mind if we join you?' Peter asked. 'Or are you expecting someone?'

No, she said, she wasn't expecting anyone and would welcome their company. Peter fetched another vodka and introduced himself and Andrew by their Christian names. Hers, she told them, was Lucy — Mrs Lucy Fillol — and she worked in the kitchens of the local hospital, although that week she was on holiday. Peter tried to lead the conversation round to her husband, but she continued to talk about herself. As the evening progressed they learned that she liked pop music, the 'Carry On' films and Bingo, and was a keen follower of television soap operas, among which Coronation Street and Crossroads ranked high. She wasn't interested in politics or sport, although occasionally she watched wrestling on ITV. Any form of ceremonial fascinated her, particularly those involving the Royal Family, whom she greatly admired. She liked cooking but not housework, and enjoyed an occasional evening in the pub. 'Friday's the big night here,' she told them. 'We come most Fridays.'

'We?' Peter prompted hopefully.

'Yes. There's usually a group or a singsong or something Fridays.'

'We must remember that,' Andrew said. 'Eh, Peter?'

Peter nodded, silently cursing him for obstructing the opening and allowing her to go off the boil, which she promptly did. What made it all the more annoying was that he knew Andrew was kidding. A group or a singsong wasn't his cup of tea at all; with Andrew drinking, like eating, was a serious business. He could consume vast quantities of ale; now, for instance, he was on his fifth pint and showed no sign of flagging. Peter envied his apparently hollow legs. A couple of pints was Peter's limit, after which it was spirits or a fractured bladder. And his capacity for spirits wasn't so hot. He was already beginning to feel high, and this was only his third whisky.

Lucy Fillol, it seemed, was more in Andrew's class than his. A constant supply of vodka had neither slurred her speech nor, apparently, clouded her mind. Peter had hoped that drink would loosen her tongue and make her less circumspect, but although she had largely monopolised the conversation there had been no hint of anything that could be construed even remotely as being connected with the kidnapping. Yet it was difficult to accept that she might have no knowledge of it, particularly as throughout the evening she had avoided all reference to her husband. The alternative, that they were on a bum steer, that Fillol was completely innocent, was not merely difficult to accept, it was impossible to accept. There were too many pointers to his guilt.

He finished his whisky and shook his head to clear it. 'About time we were moving, Andrew,' he said. Buying vodkas for Lucy Fillol was clearly a loss-making exercise. 'How about you, Lucy? Are you staying, or can we give you a lift?'

'Thanks,' she said. 'I'd like a lift. But you boys have been buying me drinks all evening. Before we go you're going to have one with me. No, really' — as they started to protest. 'I insist.' She took a fiver from her handbag. 'Get them for me, Andy, will you? I want to powder my nose. And tell Ed to make them doubles.'

Andrew grinned and looked at Peter. Peter shrugged. 'Why not?' the gesture implied. He knew that the alcohol content in his blood was well past the legal limit for anyone driving a car; but whereas the knowledge had bothered him a couple of drinks back, now it bothered him not at all. Drunk or sober, he believed himself to be a competent driver who could handle a car with the best of them; it would be his bad luck, but certainly not his fault, if some incompetent idiot involved him in an accident and the police were called. And as he would then be booked anyway another whisky could make no difference. Might as well be hanged for a sheep as for a lamb.

When Andrew returned with the drinks Lucy hitched her chair closer to him, one hand on his knee as he gave her the change. She made it clear that she was attracted to him and her voice took on a warmer note when she spoke. Already, when she wasn't calling him 'love', she had shortened his name to 'Andy', a diminutive which Andrew detested but which he presumably now suffered in what he considered to be the cause of duty. Peter was still Peter, however, and although she was friendly towards him — he too was 'love' — her friendliness lacked the hint of sexual warmth that was evident in her attitude towards Andrew. Initially Peter had been piqued by her preference. Not that he wanted her attention; but he was unused to playing second fiddle or no fiddle at all, and particularly to an untidy, hairy red ape of a man like Andrew. But the pique soon vanished, to be replaced by an amusement not unconnected with the grimaces Andrew gave him when the woman wasn't looking.

Both he and Andrew had been cautiously discreet in their probing, anxious not to alert her to the purpose behind it, but by the time Peter had finished that final whisky caution and discretion no longer seemed important. He forgot that indiscretion could put

Cathie in jeopardy, that if Fillol learned of their investigation he would assume it had been instigated by Hackett and that Hackett had no intention of paying the ransom. He was filled with a sense of power, of mastery of the situation. He had this absolute conviction that any decision he might make and any action he might take would be right. Not only right, but successful. And now was the time for action. Pussyfooting around had got them nowhere. They had to be more positive in their approach.

It was with this new sense of authority that he ushered the woman into the back of the Herald and, when Andrew made to occupy the front passenger seat, suggested he should join her. 'I'm sure Lucy would prefer to have company,' he said. 'Eh, Lucy?'

She laughed. 'Why not?'

Andrew was left with no alternative but to comply, but the look he gave Peter was far from friendly; and when Peter deliberately drove past the end of Witney Lane he was not surprised that it was Andrew and not the woman who pointed out his apparent error.

'You've missed the turning,' Andrew said sharply.

'Who cares?' Had Lucy given them her address? Peter couldn't remember. But if Andrew had made a gaffe she did not comment. 'It's a nice night for a drive. All right with you, Lucy?'

'Fine, love,' she said. 'I'm in no hurry.'

Peter grinned, aware that this was yet another move of which Andrew would disapprove. Or would he? Would the near gallon of ale that Andrew had consumed rouse him sufficiently not only to accept the situation but actually to take advantage of it? Lucy Fillol was no beauty, but that would not be evident in the dark; and although she was too flat-chested for Peter's taste her figure otherwise wasn't bad. He was tempted to prolong the journey, and he selected turnings at random, with no idea where they might lead; and although Lucy must have known the district she did not remark on the peculiar pattern of their progress, which suggested her attention was concentrated elsewhere. Then some ten minutes later the road he was following came to a dead end, with a railway embankment on one side and allotments on the other. It seemed ideal for the show-down he had in mind, and he let the Herald drift to a stop and cut the engine.

There was movement on the back seat. 'What's this?' Andrew demanded. He sounded hoarse. 'Why are we stopping here? It's a load of nothing.'

'I know.' Peter switched on the interior light and turned to face them. 'But it's quiet, and I thought we ought to have a chat.'

'Oh?' Andrew sounded surprised. 'About what?'

'Yes,' Lucy echoed. 'About what, love?'

'About Cathie Hackett,' Peter said.

Andrew whistled softly, but there was no indication that the name meant anything to the woman. 'Who's Cathie Hackett?' she asked, her tone completely casual.

'Oh, come off it, Lucy! You know damned well who she is.'

'I do?' She smiled. 'Then I suppose I

must have forgotten. But then that's me. I'm terrible with names. Tell me about her, love.'

'No,' Peter said. 'You tell us. What's happened to her? Where is she being held?'

'Happened to her? How would I know what's happened to her? I don't know her, do I?' She leaned forward to peer at him. In the weak light her long face looked colourless. 'You sure you're feeling all right, love? Maybe you shouldn't have mixed them drinks.' Before Peter could answer she turned to Andrew. 'What's he on about, Andy? Do you know? It's double-Dutch to me.'

Andrew had recovered from the jolt Peter's sudden direct approach had given him, and had his brain not been somewhat dulled by alcohol he might have rejected it in principle. But since the question had been put he saw no option but to go along with it.

'He's on about Cathie Hackett,' he said. 'She was kidnapped Monday morning. We're trying to find her.'

'Gee, but I'm sorry!' Lucy said. 'How

80

dreadful! A friend of yours, is she?'

'Yes. And we think your husband had something to do with it.'

'We don't think, we know,' Peter said. He felt a need for fresh air and wound down the window. 'And so do you, Lucy.'

'I'm sorry,' she said, 'but I don't. Honest. I mean, he couldn't have.' She settled back on the seat, apparently unruffled. 'Whatever gave you that idea?'

'A photograph.' Peter took the two photographs from his pocket. They slid from his fingers to scatter on the floor. Realising that in that light she would be unable to distinguish faces, he left them there. 'We've got a photograph that shows him meeting her. Satisfied?'

'A photograph? Honest?' She started to giggle. 'Oh, come off it, love. Pull the other one.'

It was her amusement rather than her intransigence that roused his anger. Defiance was one thing, mockery another. Had she been a man they might, however reluctantly, have threatened or even used force. But how did one compel a woman to talk against her will?

81

A late night train trundled south along the embankment, cascading sparks. In silence they watched it disappear round the bend. Then Andrew said gloomily, 'Why don't we call it a day, Peter? Take her home. She isn't going to talk. Are you, Lucy?'

'Look, love.' She sat up and put a hand on his knee. The giggles had subsided, but there was still a hint of amusement in her voice. 'I'm real sorry about your friend, and if I could help I would. But I can't tell you what I don't know, can I? So don't let's spoil a nice evening. Just take me home, eh?'

Peter shook his head. It was a gesture of frustration rather than of denial. Take her home, and what would be the outcome? She would relay their conversation to her husband, the two of them would have a bit of a giggle at his and Andrew's expense, and they would then get on with the business of squeezing Hackett. They would know that only the police could sort them out and that if Hackett had any thought of bringing in the police he would have done so days ago. As for Andrew and himself — well, no doubt they would be dismissed as a couple of interfering bunglers who had got lucky with a photograph but who had neither the ingenuity nor the gumption to finish what they had started. And they would be right. To take the woman home now would be to admit defeat.

The prospect increased Peter's anger and hardened his resolve. Sod them! he thought. If the stupid cow thinks she's got us beat she's bloody well mistaken. For a start, we'll see how the bastards like a taste of their own medicine.

Without a word he switched off the interior light, started the engine, reversed into the opposite pavement and accelerated back down the road with all the speed the Herald could muster. The movement was so sudden and so furious that the two on the back seat, caught unawares, were thrown off balance.

'Watch it, man!' Andrew protested, righting himself. 'What's the hurry?'

Peter ignored the protest. He drove fast, tyres screaming as the car skidded round corners. But speed had nothing to do with anger. Anger had gone when he made his decision. It was delight in his own ingenuity, bolstered by alcohol, that excited him now, and he needed speed to express his excitement. He grinned to himself in anticipation of the woman's reaction when she learned what he had in mind.

He had only a vague notion of the route he had taken before parking by the allotments, and he kept heading west until he hit the main road. Not yet completely sober, but sober enough to remember that main roads were the haunt of police cars, he reduced speed and drove on towards Lewisham.

'What's with you, man?' Andrew shouted. 'You've done it again, dammit! You've passed the bloody turning.'

'I know,' Peter said.

'Why?'

'Yes, why?' Lucy echoed. 'I thought you were taking me home.'

'I am,' Peter said.

'But it's back there.'

'Not your home, Lucy. Ours. You're coming with us.'

Andrew gasped. 'Are you crazy? What the hell for?'

Lucy laughed. 'Well, I may be past the chicken stage, but if I say it myself I'm in pretty good shape. It's all there and in working order. So if that's what you're after, love — '

'It isn't,' Peter said. He had thought to hear a hint of nervousness in her laughter. 'You don't have to worry on that score.'

'Oh, I'm not worried,' she said. 'Not with two such nice boys for company.'

Andrew leaned forward to grip Peter's shoulder. 'Don't be a bloody fool, Peter,' he pleaded. 'Take her back. We don't need that sort of trouble.'

'We need a hostage.' Lights turned to red before Peter could stop, and he accelerated away, trusting no police car had been lurking up a side street. 'They pinch one of ours, we pinch one of theirs. Tit for tat.'

'Go easy on the pinching,' Lucy said. 'I bruise easily.'

Andrew was unhappy about the scheme and expressed his concern forcibly. Tit for tat was all very well, he said, but not when it came to kidnapping. Kidnapping was a major crime, they were putting themselves in conflict with the Law. Theoretically that might be true, Peter agreed; but Fillol and his boys were in no position to call in the police, so forget the Law. All right, Andrew said impatiently, forget it. But they were dealing with criminals, men who could be dangerous. Did Peter really believe they would settle for a straight swap and kiss the ransom goodbye? 'Will they hell!' Andrew said. 'They'll come looking for us, that's what. They'll bloody well sort us out.'

'How can they? They don't know who we are or where to find us.'

'Oh, be your age, Peter! If they don't now they bloody soon will. They'll know we must be connected with Ben. Put the frighteners on him, and if the pressure's right he'll talk. And who could blame him?'

'He won't know it's us. Not if we keep her well hidden.'

'He doesn't have to know. He'll guess. Who else could it be?' Peter did not answer, he didn't know who else. 'Cut it out, Peter. Let's take her back.'

The argument continued, with Peter stubbornly refusing to give way. He knew that much of what Andrew said made sense, and had he been completely sober at the moment of decision he might have decided differently. But he was in no mood to change his mind now. Having come so far they had to go on. If it didn't work out, if the situation looked like getting out of hand, they could always release the woman before anyone got hurt.

Lucy listened without comment. An occasional giggle suggested that she found the situation diverting, and she seemed particularly amused at their references to her husband. But by now Peter had become used to her apparent unconcern. She should have been angry, indignant, frightened, and that she showed none of these emotions indicated that she was considerably tougher than she looked. Not that it mattered. Her reaction had little bearing on the situation. Whether she liked it or not, they had her. She was their bargaining power.

By the time they reached Hamble

Close, Andrew had abandoned the argument, resigned to the knowledge that with Peter in the driving seat, metaphorically as well as literally, he had been fighting a losing battle. All right, he told Peter, we'll play it your way. But I still think it's crazy, and ten to one it'll go sour on us.

Lucy accompanied them into the flat without protest, and nodded approvingly as she surveyed the sitting-room. 'Nice,' she said. 'I like large rooms. Seems to make breathing easier, if you know what I mean. In Witney Lane they're really tiny. Like boxes. But you could do with some new furniture, couldn't you? This lot looks like it came out of the Ark.'

'It's not considered good manners for a guest to criticise,' Peter said. He was feeling more kindly disposed towards her, realising that her cheerful acceptance of the situation made their task easier. Had she been a screamer, had she kicked up an almighty row, it would have been next to impossible to conceal her presence from Ben and Harry. 'But you're right, of course. It's pretty ropey.

I hope it won't spoil your stay.'

'Oh, it won't do that, love.' She made herself comfortable on the settee. 'But if I'm a guest and not a prisoner, how about offering me a drink? Vodka, for preference.'

'No vodka,' Andrew said.

'All right, then, gin. With lime.'

'Sorry. No gin and no lime. Just whisky or beer.'

'Whisky, please,' she said. 'Any ginger ale?'

'No,' Andrew said, 'no ginger ale. Straight or with water.'

She chose to drink it straight. Andrew poured whisky for the three of them. Watching Peter flick over the pages of his notebook, she said, 'What happens now? I mean, something happens, doesn't it?'

'I'm going to telephone your husband,' Peter said.

'You are?' She smiled. 'You know the number?'

'Of course. It's in the book.'

'Is it really?' The smile broadened. 'Amazing! May I speak to him.'

'That depends,' Peter said, dialling.

A woman answered his call. When he asked to speak to Fillol she hesitated. It was late, she said, Mr Fillol was in bed. Couldn't it wait till morning? No, Peter said, it couldn't, the matter was urgent. Hang on then, she said, while I fetch him.

He had to wait a couple of minutes. Then a man's voice said, 'Daniel Fillol here. Who's speaking?'

'Never mind who's speaking,' Peter said. 'I thought you'd like to know that we've kidnapped your wife and — '

'You've what?'

'We've kidnapped your wife,' Peter repeated. 'You can have her back when Mrs Hackett is returned to her husband. And you can forget the ransom. That's out. Understood?'

There was a moment's silence. Then the man said sharply, 'No, it bloody isn't. I don't go for sick jokes, mister. Not at this hour.' And rang off.

Furious, Peter dialled again. 'Listen!' he snapped when the man answered. 'This is no joke, Fillol. I tell you, we've got your wife, and if you don't believe me you can speak to her. But first — '

'No, damn you, you listen!' the man interrupted. 'I don't know what your game is, but I know you haven't got my wife. And for why? Because it was my wife who answered the telephone, and she's standing beside me right now. So bugger off, damn you, and let me get some sleep!'

7

Stunned into temporary silence, Peter replaced the receiver and turned to look at the woman. She was still smiling, and for the first time he noticed that she had slightly buck teeth. Inconsequentially he wondered why he had not noticed that before.

'Well?' she demanded. Despite the smile there was defiance in her tone, as if she were a child expecting a reprimand. 'What did he say?'

'He said that you're not his wife, that she was there with him in the room.' Peter fought to restrain his anger. 'So who the devil are you?'

'I told you. I'm Lucy Fillol.'

'But not Daniel Fillol's wife?'

'No.'

'Then why did you say you were?'

'I didn't, love. You assumed it. Daniel's my brother-in-law. My husband's been dead for years.'

'You led us to assume it,' Peter persisted. 'When we referred to your husband as if he were alive you didn't deny it. Why?'

She shrugged. 'Men seem to shy away from widows. Know what I mean? They think we're on the make.' The smile was back. 'I had to laugh when you said you'd got a photograph of my husband meeting this girl who's been kidnapped. I mean, I know people say they've taken photographs of the dead — spirit photographs, isn't it? — but I don't believe in that sort of thing, do you?' The smile broadened. 'It was even funnier when you said his number was in the book.'

Munching through a packet of savoury biscuits, Andrew had listened to the conversation with growing astonishment and concern. 'Are you saying we've kidnapped the wrong woman?' he demanded, crumbs sprinkling his beard.

'Well, if you thought I was Daniel's wife — yes, love, I'm afraid you have. Sorry.'

'But we saw you go in and out of

Number 57. And that's Daniel's house.'

'You mean you were watching me?'

'Not you,' Peter said curtly. 'The house. But you came out at a quarter to two and went back an hour later. And as you had a key we assumed you lived there.'

'Well, I don't. I live at Number 25. Top flat.' She finished her whisky and leaned back to put the glass on the table. 'Only I was spending today with Grace because she wasn't feeling too good. She had one of her turns.'

'Grace is Daniel's wife?' Lucy nodded. 'And you have a key to their house?'

'No, of course I don't. Daniel wouldn't stand for that. It was just that Grace wanted some aspirin and she lent me a key to get back in.' A prolonged yawn stretched her face still further. 'They sell aspirin in pubs. Did you know that?'

They sell booze too, Peter thought, which is no doubt what kept you so long.

'Funny you're not listed in the telephone directory,' he said. He made it sound like an accusation. 'Or aren't you on the phone?'

'Yes. But it's a pay phone, and it's listed

94

under Trakos, the couple who own the house. They live in the bottom flat.' After a pause she added. 'They're Cypriots. Nice, though.'

At the back of Peter's mind lurked the thought that if Ben Hackett and Daniel Fillol were cousins, and if Lucy had been married to Daniel's brother, she should know Ben. Would it be politic to ask her? Whatever the answer, could it be of value? To put the question would be to expose his knowledge of Hackett's true identity and the relationship between the two men. Would that be wise? Uncertain of the pros and cons, he kept silent.

Andrew refilled the glasses and offered Lucy a biscuit, which she refused. 'There's one thing I don't understand,' he said. 'If you knew we had you wrong, why didn't you correct us when Peter asked you about Cathie Hackett?'

She shrugged. 'I don't know. No, that's not true — I do know. You see, if you'd known I wasn't Daniel's wife you'd have taken me home at once, wouldn't you? I didn't want that. I was enjoying myself.'

'You mean you *wanted* to be kidnapped?'

'Well, no. I mean, I didn't know it was going to happen, did I? You didn't know yourself; not till we were on the way here. Then — well, it was exciting, and a woman living on her own doesn't get much excitement. I know I don't.'

Was she really as innocent as she claimed to be? Peter wondered. She had given apparently reasonable answers to all their questions, and if some of her behaviour seemed unlikely from his way of thinking it could well be in character for her. She wasn't exactly a run-of-the-mill pick-up. And yet . . .

'Well, anyway, your precious brother-in-law is definitely involved in Cathie Hackett's disappearance,' he said. 'There's no mistake about that. And you live in the same street and visit his house. It seems strange you know nothing about it.'

'Well, I don't. And it isn't strange either. For one thing, if he *has* kidnapped your friend — and I'm quite sure he hasn't — he isn't keeping her at Number

57. I should know, shouldn't I? I helped Grace with the housework only yesterday.'

'We didn't think he was.'

'Then why watch the house? Spying on Daniel, were you?'

'You might say that,' Peter agreed. 'What's the other thing?'

'Eh? Oh, yes. Well, Daniel and I don't get on. That's why I usually only visit Grace when he's out. If Daniel was up to something I'm the last person he'd tell.'

'Why?' Andrew asked. 'Why don't you get on?'

'That's personal, love.'

'So you don't think he'd be prepared to hand Cathie over in exchange for you?' Peter asked.

She laughed. 'Not a hope, love. Given the choice I reckon he'd prefer for you to keep me.'

'What does he do for a living?'

'He's a partner in a scrapyard.'

Andrew screwed up the empty biscuit carton and threw it at the wastepaper basket, which he missed. 'That's that, then, isn't it?' he said. 'We ballsed it up.'

'Looks like it, love.'

'So one of us had better run you home. Eh, Peter?'

'Of course,' Peter said.

'Oh, no, you don't!' Glass in hand, Lucy swung her feet on to the settee and lay back. 'Not at this hour. I'm not being shoved around like a blooming dummy. Here I am and here I stay. For tonight, anyway.'

'But we've only the two beds,' Peter protested.

'Then two of us will have to double up, won't we?' she said cheerfully. Peter wondered if the look she gave Andrew was indicative of who she thought the two should be. 'Anyway, when you started this lark you were planning to keep me here, weren't you? So where did you expect me to sleep?'

'I hadn't thought about it, I'm afraid,' Peter admitted. 'It was a spur of the moment thing.'

'Then you'd better think about it now, love. It's long past my bedtime.'

They thought about it. In the end Peter gave up his room. He would sleep on the settee, he said; the balls-up was of his making and he should be the one to suffer. Lucy said he almost certainly would. The settee was not only uncomfortable, it was also small for a man of his size; his feet would stick out at one end and his head at the other. Maybe she had better stay where she was, she said, it was more her size than his. Now on his third whisky, Andrew protested that as their guest a makeshift cot was not for her; if it was too small for Peter, maybe they should reconsider her suggestion about doubling up. Peter couldn't decide whether or not he was serious. Lucy, however, seemed in no doubt that he was. Her hitherto provocative manner deserted her and she said, almost primly, that she was out of practice in double bunking and she suspected Andrew might snore. Bearded men usually did. If they wouldn't let her sleep on the settee, she said, she would accept Peter's offer of his bed. And not to worry with pyjamas, she said, she slept raw.

Peter awoke the next morning with an aching back, cold feet and a stiff neck. His stomach didn't feel too good either, and he had a headache. He threw off the blankets and sat on the edge of the settee, holding his head in his hands. Presently he became aware of the smell of coffee and frying bacon, and he padded barefooted into the hall. He could hear Andrew in the bathroom — Andrew didn't sing or whistle in the bath, but kept up an intermittent grunting noise — and he went down the hall to the open door of the kitchen. The table was laid for breakfast, and Lucy sat at one end, eating toast and with a copy of the *Daily Telegraph* propped against the coffee-pot.

She smiled when she saw him. 'Hello, there!' she said brightly. 'You look a weeny bit rough. Didn't sleep too well, eh?'

'Not too well,' he admitted, staring at her. She looked different. More sedate, less conspicuous. Then he noticed her hair. It was no longer auburn but a dark brown, cut close to the head, with a peak at the nape of the neck and a narrow fringe in front. 'Were you wearing a wig last night?'

'Yes. Didn't you notice? It's good, isn't

it? Very natural. I wear it most evenings.'

He sat down, twisting his neck to loosen it, and poured coffee. 'You shouldn't have bothered to get breakfast,' he said. 'We could have done that.'

'No bother, love. Andy said you usually have a cooked breakfast, so I've done bacon and eggs. Is that all right?'

'Not for me, thanks. My stomach isn't up to it. I'll stick to toast. But it won't be wasted. Andrew will get through a double portion with no trouble at all.'

She passed him the newspaper. 'I haven't opened it,' she said. 'Just peeped inside, that's all. I know men don't like having their papers messed up. But it's terribly dull, isn't it? I prefer the *Sun* or the *Daily Mirror*.'

Andrew joined them, fresh from his bath, and tackled the double portion of bacon and eggs without comment. The plate empty, he leaned back and produced his customary belch.

'That's better,' he said, and patted his stomach.

'So I hear,' Lucy said, eyeing the traces of egg on his beard. 'Still, better out than in, I suppose. Toast?'

'Please.' He reached for the butter. 'Amazing how one's appetite improves when someone else does the cooking.'

'Yours couldn't improve,' Peter said. 'Your capacity is infinite, and one can't improve on that.' He poured more coffee, drank it and stood up. 'Give me a few minutes to get dressed, Lucy, and I'll run you home.'

'Not home, love,' she said. 'The station will do nicely, thanks.'

He protested that to drive her home was the least recompense he could make for the inconvenience, not to mention the apprehension, they had caused her. She dismissed the protest with a smile. There was no need for recompense or apology, she said; the experience was one she was glad not to have missed and she had enjoyed every minute of it. Or almost every minute. Nor was there any need to drive her home. She had planned to shop in the West End that morning, and she could do that as easily from Wimbledon as from Lewisham. He offered her a lift to Town, but she rejected that too. 'No offence, love, but I prefer the train,' she said. 'It's more restful.'

He took her to the station and bought copies of the *Sun* and the *Daily Mirror*. He wanted to buy flowers, but she pointed out that shopping in London carrying a large bouquet really wasn't on. 'Don't forget to look in at the Squirrel when you're down that way,' she said as they parted. 'I'm there most evenings, though I don't usually stay late except on Fridays.'

He promised that they would, and knew that it was a promise neither he nor Andrew was likely to keep. The knowledge made him feel guilty.

On his return to the flat he was surprised to find Andrew watering the plants in the conservatory. Having bought the damned things you should bloody well look after them, Andrew said, and you didn't water them yesterday, did you? Water them daily, Peter said, and you'll drown them. 'Once a week would be ample, the man said, and some of them — I can't remember which — even less.'

'Well, that's a relief,' Andrew said. He

returned to the sitting-room and practically fell into an armchair, the springs protesting noisily. 'Lucy safely away by courtesy of British Rail, is she?'

'Yes.'

'Good.' Andrew took his pipe from his pocket and began to fill it. 'So what's the next move? Pass the information to Ben and leave him to get on with it?'

Pointless, Peter said. Coals to Newcastle. Hackett must have known from the start that his cousin was involved — hence his lack of interest in the photograph — yet apparently he still preferred to try and meet the ransom demand rather than go to the police. 'Though God knows why. There could be no risk to Cathie. Once Fillol was arrested the others wouldn't dare to harm her.'

'He doesn't know *we* know. It might force his hand if he did.'

'Perhaps.' It was a step Peter was reluctant to take, it would mean the end of adventure for himself. 'But let's see if we can take it a bit further first.'

'How?'

'Fillol must visit wherever Cathie is being held. If we keep a discreet watch on Number 57 he might lead us there.'

'Oh, no!' Andrew caught the pipe as it dropped from his mouth. 'I've had surveillance, thank you! Anyway, I'm busy this afternoon. An ad for a new deodorant. And don't say it smells.'

'I won't. Am I expected to act as chauffeur?'

'No. The garage rang while you were out. The car will be ready after lunch.'

'Good. Then I'll survey on my own.'

'After you've run me to the garage, eh?' Andrew said.

They lunched out. As they munched their way through steak and chips it occurred to Peter that to swap cars with Andrew for the afternoon might be a wise move. When Lucy got home she would almost certainly recount her adventure to Grace, and Grace would pass it on to her husband; which meant that Fillol would be on the look-out for further interference. He had seen the Triumph in Witney Lane, had nearly collided with it. If he were to see it there again he could well be suspicious and would take no action that might impair the success of his scheme.

Andrew wasn't keen on the exchange but agreed to make it, and Peter drove down to Witney Lane, parked some thirty yards up the hill from Number 57, and settled down to wait. The white Morris Traveller, which he had assumed was Fillol's — he should have asked Lucy about that — was again outside the house, so either Fillol was at home or the scrapyard was within easy walking distance. He considered trying to locate it — could Cathie be there? — and decided otherwise. It was unlikely he could search the yard, let alone any buildings, without being spotted, and he might well miss Fillol while he was away.

Dusk had fallen when Fillol came walking up the hill and went into Number 57. Peter continued to wait, hoping that when the man had eaten his supper or his tea or whatever he called it he might decide to visit an accomplice, perhaps even Cathie. And forty minutes later his vigil was rewarded. A man came out from Number 57, and although it was now too dark to identify him positively as Fillol the fact that he unlocked the Morris Traveller and got into the driving seat was proof enough for Peter. When the Morris moved off down the hill he waited until it was nearing the main road and then went after it.

The Morris kept to main roads, turning right at Catford and continuing through Norwood in a southerly direction. Peter stayed close, trusting in the traffic to conceal him from his quarry. Approaching Croydon, however, the near side indicator on the Morris started to blink and he dropped back, aware that to turn down a side street right on Fillol's heels would invite suspicion. The street was residential, running between small, tightly packed semi-detached villas, and as Peter turned into it he saw the Morris slow to a stop some fifty yards ahead. He drove on past to park at what he considered to be a safe distance and walked cautiously back. There was no sign of Fillol, who had presumably gone into one of the houses. But with so many cars lining the street it did not have to be the house opposite the

Morris. Playing safe, he returned to wait beside the Cortina.

Fillol did not keep him waiting long. Ten minutes after he had gone in he came out, accompanied by another man. They stood conferring on the pavement before getting into the Morris, and by the light of a nearby street lamp Peter recognised Fillol's companion as the man he had spoken to the previous Saturday outside the flat; the man, for want of a name, he and Andrew referred to as 'the Warren man'. This, then, was another of the kidnappers. Presumably he had been in Hamble Close that afternoon to check on the Hacketts, although the reason seemed obscure. The way the kidnapping had been engineered did not suggest a need for any particular knowledge of their lifestyle, and certainly not knowledge that could be got by peering through a hedge.

The Morris came on down the street, headlights dipped, and Peter crouched behind the Cortina until it was past. Then he slid into the driving seat and went after it. Soon they were back on the Croydon Road and heading south again, and when the Morris turned right on to the bypass Peter felt the adrenalin begin to flow. It flowed faster still when they took the Brighton road. He was as certain as if they had told him that they were on their way to where Cathie was being held.

They were through Purley and well down the Brighton road when the Morris turned off. Peter slowed, and followed the glow of its headlights as the road twisted and turned, heading into a countryside that was foreign to him. Soon they were in narrow lanes, with low hedges and patches of woodland, and only an occasional cottage or farm building to show that the district was not completely uninhabited. Peter dipped his headlights and dropped back still further. By now Fillol must be aware that another car was behind him; a few more miles and surely, knowing what Lucy had told him, he would begin to suspect the truth. He was still dropping back when the lights ahead vanished, and he switched the Cortina's lights to full beam and accelerated round the next bend. There was no sign of the Morris, and his first thought was that he had been rumbled and that somehow Fillol had managed to give him the slip. Then, among the trees to his left and about a hundred yards ahead, he saw a faint glow of light and guessed that the Morris had been driven off the road. His immediate impulse was to stop, and his foot was already on the brake pedal when he realised that to stop would create greater suspicion than to go on. He released the brake and drove on slowly. The Morris had been parked down a rough track through the trees, its side lights on. From his brief glimpse of it as he passed he was unable to see whether the two men were in or out of the car, but they would not have parked merely for a rest or a smoke. This was the end of the journey. Somewhere down the track a no doubt frightened Cathie would be imprisoned.

He parked the Cortina at the first available spot that allowed him to get the car off the road and hurried back. The Morris was only a few yards down the track, and by its lights he saw that beyond it was a wide field gate, and beyond the gate an expanse of grazing land. He approached the car cautiously. Through the rear windows he could see that it was unoccupied, and he went past it to the gate and stood peering into the darkness ahead. Moon and stars peeped furtively through high drifting clouds, and away on the horizon the crest of the South Downs merged with the sky; below that was blackness, relieved only by the faint lights shining from distant windows. The only sounds were those of the wind in the trees and the hum of cars on a distant highway.

Satisfied that he was alone, he climbed the gate and started along the track, not knowing where it might end but hopeful that it would lead him to Cathie. Progress was uneven. The track was deeply rutted, the ground hard through lack of rain, and he stumbled often. He kept pausing to listen, and when his eyes grew more accustomed to the dark he discerned the vague outlines of a building some twenty yards ahead. Stepping carefully to avoid making a noise he moved closer. The building was a large wooden barn, with wide double doors and a high roof; the doors were open, which suggested that the men had gone inside. But there was no sound, and that puzzled him. Unless they talked in the faintest of whispers — and why would they do that? — from where he stood he should hear them. There was no light either, yet surely they would have had a torch? What were they doing in the silent dark? Or had he misread the situation? He had assumed that because the Morris was parked by the gate and the gate gave access to the track, that must be the way they had gone; and that because the track led to the barn the barn had been their destination. But the assumption could be wrong. They could have parked by the gate because that happened to be the nearest available space. From there they could have gone in any direction, although the open gate suggested they had gone south rather than north. Even if they had used the track they might not have been making for the barn. They could have continued past it to some further destination.

Reluctantly he accepted the fact that

the first step must be to determine whether or not the men were inside the barn. If they were, then his appearance could be the introduction to a punch-up from which he would almost certainly emerge the loser. Yet he had to know, and he approached the open doorway, ears cocked for any indication of danger, and peered cautiously inside. It was even darker inside than out, the men could be there and he would not see them; but there was no rustle of movement, no sound other than his own breathing. He turned and looked back up the track. The lights of the Morris still showed, the men had to be somewhere in the vicinity. So what did he do? Go back to the gate, hide among the trees, and wait for the men to return? He could note the direction from which they came. But that could be misleading; they might not return direct, and he could not search the countryside in the dark. Better to clear out and return in the morning, preferably with Andrew to help in the search. Cathie could not be far. Given time and persistence they should be able to find her.

He reached for his lighter to get a cursory view of the inside of the barn before leaving. Then something heavy and yielding descended on the back of his head and he fell heavily into unconsciousness.

8

Peter got to his knees and tenderly explored the back of his aching head. He could feel no swelling and no open wound, which suggested that whatever his assailant had used as a weapon it had stunned rather than bludgeoned him into unconsciousness. Relieved, he stood up and leant against the doorpost, waiting for a sudden attack of nausea to pass. He had no idea how long he had been unconscious; but it must have been at least several minutes, for the lights of the Morris no longer showed beyond the gate, implying that the men had gone. He took out his lighter, switched it to full flame, and held it high to inspect the interior of the barn. The distant corners were beyond his field of vision, but he got the impression that it was more or less derelict. The floor was covered liberally with several inches of straw, a few bales were stacked against the wall to his right.

Planks were missing from the far wall and glass from the windows, and when he looked up he could see the sky through a large hole in the roof. Near his feet were a few small bags of sand, and his head swam as he bent to pick one up. It was heavier than it looked. He guessed that it was one of these his assailant had used as a weapon.

'Cathie!' he called.

There was no answer, not even an echo. He did not bother to explore further. This was no place to hold a prisoner, not even temporarily. So why had the men come? They must have had a purpose, but what it might be was beyond his comprehension.

When he felt sufficiently recovered he made his way back to the gate, every involuntary stumble causing a spasm of pain to shoot through his head. The gate was shut now, and he climbed it and walked down the road to the Cortina. In his haste to follow the men he had not bothered to lock it, and he eased himself into the driving seat and switched on the engine. As soon as the car started to move the feel of the steering wheel told him he was in trouble. Resigned to a puncture, he got out and examined the off-side front tyre. It wasn't merely punctured, it was completely flat, and when he felt for the valve he found that the cap was off and the core missing. A further inspection revealed that two other tyres had received similar treatment. But why? Why bother to immobilise him when by now they could be miles away and in no danger of his spying on their movements? It seemed as pointless as their visit to the barn.

Anger seized him, and he lashed out at a wheel with his foot, wincing at the stab of pain that shot up his leg as the foot connected with metal. Then he locked the car and limped off up the lane in search of help.

★   ★   ★

It was well after midnight when he drove into Hamble Close and parked behind the Triumph. Number 3 was in darkness, and he let himself into the flat and went into the kitchen. It looked remarkably tidy, which suggested that Andrew had dined out; left to himself, Andrew seldom bothered to clear away the dishes after the evening meal, let alone wash them up. Peter boiled milk and cut himself a cheese sandwich, and took them down the hall to his room. Holding the sandwich between his teeth to give himself a free hand, he opened the door and switched on the light. A couple of paces into the room and he halted in astonishment. For a moment he thought that the sandbag had impaired his vision, and he shook his head to clear it. But there was no mistake. A hump under the bedclothes indicated that the bed was occupied.

He took the sandwich from his mouth. 'Bloody hell!' he exclaimed. 'What's going on?'

The figure in the bed started to stir, with only the dark tip of its hair visible. Peter did not wait for it to materialise fully. He slapped sandwich and mug down on the bedside table, reached for the bedclothes, and yanked them away in one swift movement. They were over the foot of the bed before he realised that the figure was that of a naked female.

'Jesus!' he said, hopelessly embarrassed. 'I didn't know. I mean I — sorry!'

It took Lucy Fillol a few seconds to come awake to what had happened. Then she wriggled down the bed on her bottom, reached for the bedclothes, and wrapped them untidily around her. Only then did she turn to look at the intruder. But Peter wasn't waiting for recognition or an explanation. He shot out of the room, closed the door, and leant against it to recover his composure. Then he marched into Andrew's room, switched on the light, and shook him awake.

'What the — !' Andrew rolled over and blinked at him. 'Oh, it's you!'

'What the hell's that woman doing in my bed?' Peter demanded.

'Sleeping, I imagine. Or did you disturb her?' Andrew yawned, lifted himself on to an elbow, and reached for his wristwatch. 'Christ! It's after midnight. What kept you?'

'Never mind what kept me. I want to know what Lucy's doing here.'

'Ah!' Still yawning, Andrew sat up,

arched his back, and scratched the back of his head. 'Well, she just turned up. I got back around six and there she was: stretched out on the settee with a glass of vodka and tonic, watching the telly.'

'We haven't got any vodka.'

'We have now. She brought a bottle with her.'

'But if you weren't here, who let her in?'

'She let herself in. Apparently she took the spare key from the kitchen. Nicked it when she got up this morning.'

'But that means she'd planned to return even before she left.'

'Exactly.'

'Why, for God's sake?'

'She likes it here, she says.' Fully awake now, Andrew grinned. 'She likes the flat, she likes our company, she likes the neighbourhood. And since we went to so much trouble to kidnap her she reckons we must want to have her around. At least, she doesn't, of course, but that's her excuse. Anyway, apparently she went home, collected a few things, and came back this afternoon. To stay.'

'To stay? Oh, no!'

'For a day or two, she says.' Andrew stroked his beard. 'You walked in on her unannounced, did you? What did she say?'

'I didn't wait for her to say anything. I was so mad I just yanked the bedclothes off her — and there she was, completely raw.'

Andrew showed interest. 'Did you, though! How does she rate? Figure-wise, I mean.'

Peter shrugged. 'I didn't wait for a close inspection. As soon as I saw boobs I got out quick. Incidentally, I left my milk and a sandwich in there.'

'Chicken!' Andrew threw back the bedclothes. 'Well, if you're planning another sandwich I think I'll join you. We dined early.'

'We?'

'Lucy made a curry. I wouldn't know the ingredients, but it tasted terrific. She's a superb cook, I'll say that for her. Actually, she made enough for three, but as you didn't turn up we finished it between us.'

'I can imagine where most of it went,' Peter said. 'However, cook or no cook I want her out. I want to sleep in my own bed. And why didn't you warn me she was here? You could at least have left a note.'

'I did. In the living-room. And your bed's made up on the settee. Lucy wanted to kip down there herself, but seeing as you were obviously going to be late I thought it would cause less commotion if we left it for you.'

'Thoughtful of you. It didn't occur to you to let her have your bed?'

'Actually, no.' Andrew bent to put on his slippers. 'What kept you, anyway?'

Peter told him. 'I had to walk miles to get to a telephone. Or it seemed like miles. Then I had to wait while the R.A.C. organised a garage to rescue me.'

Lucy was at the stove when they reached the kitchen, wearing Peter's dressing-gown. 'I hope you don't mind me borrowing it, love,' she said, with no show of embarrassment. 'I know you've seen what little there is to see, but I don't want to push it.'

Peter said that of course he didn't mind and apologised for the intrusion. His head still ached, but much as he longed to sleep in his own bed he could not bring himself to voice his resentment at being barred from it. 'Is that my sandwich?' he asked, pointing to one on the table.

'Yes. And I'm reheating your milk.' The milk started to bubble in the saucepan. She poured it into a beaker and looked at Andrew. 'How about you, Andy? You hungry too?'

Andrew admitted that a sandwich would not come amiss. Watching her cut the bread he said, 'I'm afraid I've let you in for something tomorrow evening, Peter. My client this afternoon wants advice on choosing a prep school for his son and I promised I'd take you along to his place for a drink. That okay?'

'Why me? He'd do better with a scholastic agent.'

'I dare say.' With a nod of thanks to Lucy, Andrew bit into his sandwich. 'But talk to him, will you? He's important. Could be useful to me.'

'A drink's a drink,' Peter said. 'I'll talk to him.'

'I'll have a meal ready for when you get back, then,' Lucy said. She patted Peter on the cheek. 'Cheer up, love. Tomorrow night you can have your bed back. And that's a promise. I'll take the settee.'

Generous of you, Peter thought. Aloud he said, 'Look, Lucy. I don't want to seem rude, but aren't you carrying this a bit too far? I know we brought you here, but — '

'Include me out,' Andrew said. 'You brought her.'

'By force,' Lucy said. 'I was kidnapped, wasn't I?'

'Yes. But — '

'You said I was to stay here until your friend's wife was released.'

'I know. But — '

'All right, then. I'm staying.'

'But it was a mistake,' Peter protested. 'You know that.'

'Of course I know it. I said so, didn't I? Daniel had nothing to do with it, I said.'

'I don't mean that. I'm talking about mistaking you for his wife. We wanted you as a hostage. Now — well, it's different.'

'Now I'm just a nuisance, eh?'

'Not exactly,' Peter said. Civility forbade that he should agree. 'But the flat isn't suitable for three. Not with only the two bedrooms. Wouldn't you be more comfortable at home?'

'No, I wouldn't. And if it's not suitable, why bring me here?' Again she patted his cheek, and this time it was nearer a slap. 'One has to pay for one's mistakes, love. You know? I like it here and I needed a change. A few days away from Witney Lane will do me a power of good.' She blew Andrew a kiss. 'Goodnight, boys. Sleep tight.'

They sat in silence until they heard the bedroom door close. Then Andrew said slowly, 'I suppose she's on the level.'

'How do you mean?'

'Well, is she really here from choice, or is she spying on us for friend Daniel? Reporting back to him on what we're up to. She could use the phone while we're out.'

Impossible, Peter said. She couldn't have known they would be at the

Squirrel, and she certainly couldn't have known she was going to be kidnapped. 'No. Like she said, I think she just welcomes the change. It's an adventure, too, and I don't suppose she gets much excitement in Witney Lane. And another thing. I think she likes having a man around, someone to cook and clean up for. She's the type. Two of us must be a bonus.'

'Do you think she fancies us?'

'I think she fancies you. No taste. But don't let that give you ideas. Lucy's no push-over. Or I don't think she is. You want it, you've bloody well got to earn it.' Peter drained his beaker and put it in the sink. 'Well, I'm for the settee and the rudiments of sleep — I hope. Are you coming down to the farm with me tomorrow?'

'Is that where you're going?'

'You bet I am. I want to inspect the place in daylight.'

'I may as well,' Andrew said. 'If only to protect you from another bonk on the nut.'

They left early, after a breakfast of scrambled eggs and grilled mushrooms expertly prepared by Lucy. When, after persistent questioning, she learned that they were driving down to Sussex — but not exactly where, since Peter did not know that himself — she pleaded to be taken with them. She did not often get the chance of a drive in the country, she said. Sorry, Peter said, you don't get one now, I'm afraid; this is strictly business, passengers are out. On the other hand, if she cared for them to drop her off in Lewisham *en route*, he said, they would be happy to oblige.

No, she said, more tartly than they had hitherto heard her speak, she didn't care for that at all. And when they returned from wherever they were going, she said, they could get their own damned lunch. She had intended to prepare a loin of pork with all the trimmings, but she wasn't slaving all morning in the kitchen for such a pair of meanies. Peter pointed out that she could hardly have spent the morning slaving in the kitchen and also driving down to Sussex. In any case, he said, the slaving could be unnecessary since they might not be back for lunch.

They went in the Herald and made for

the garage which the R.A.C. had contacted on Peter's behalf the previous night. Peter found the man who had rescued him and explained that he must have dropped his lighter while examining the flat tyres; but he had only a vague idea of where the incident had occurred and could the man pin-point it for him on the map? The man could and did. 'Blest if I know how you come to be on that road, though,' he said. 'Seeing as you was making for London, I mean. Lost your way, had you?'

Peter nodded. 'I thought it looked like a short cut.'

'It's short, all right. Leads just about nowhere.' The man wiped his hands on a rag. 'You know something? You never did tell me how it happened; kept me awake, that did, trying to figure it out. I mean, there you was, parked in your motor, and someone comes along and whips out the valve centres. Just like that.' He shook his head. 'Having a kip, was you?'

'Yes.' Other than the truth, it seemed as good an explanation as any. 'I stopped to light a cigarette and must have dropped off. I'd had a hard day.'

'And you didn't hear his motor?'

'No. But then he was probably on foot.'

'Why d'you think he done it?'

'I haven't the faintest idea,' Peter said, annoyed by the man's curiosity. 'Someone with a warped sense of humour, I imagine.'

'Or drunk,' Andrew suggested.

'Yes.' Peter turned to where the Herald stood by the pumps. 'Shove in three gallons, will you? Four star.'

'Can't figure why anyone'd be walking along there that time of night,' the man said, watching the hand move round the dial. 'Like I said, it don't lead nowhere. 'Cept Warren Farm, of course. And ain't no one there would do a crazy thing like that.'

It was not until the hand had clicked into place and the man started to remove the nozzle from the tank that the possible significance of that piece of information hit Peter.

'Warren Farm?' he said sharply.

'That's right. Adam Topping's place. About a mile back from where you parked. He farms the land thereabouts. Sheep, mostly. And horses. He hires them out.'

Peter paid and drove off the forecourt. As he changed into second gear Andrew said, 'You got it too, eh? Warren Farm, I mean.'

'I got it,' Peter said.

'It could be a coincidence, I suppose.'

'It couldn't,' Peter said with conviction. 'I'll wager anything you like that Adam Topping is the chap I found snooping outside the flat last Saturday. He had to explain what he was doing there, so he invented this friend; and he gave him the first name that came into his head, which happened to be that of his farm.'

'But you said he was the man Fillol picked up in Croydon last night.'

'So he was. What of it?'

'Well, what was he doing in Croydon if he lives down here?'

'Visiting, presumably. People do. And Fillol collected him and drove him home.' Peter accelerated out of the village. 'We're on target, Andrew,' he said gleefully. 'Bang on.'

'Could be. But — Topping,' Andrew said. 'Would you say that's a fairly common name?'

'Not particularly. Why?'

'I've heard it before, that's why. Can't think where, though.'

'Like Fillol, eh?' Peter said. 'It'll be Hackett next. Or Smith.'

'Ah! Smith it might be,' Andrew said.

The garage man's directions had been explicit and they had no difficulty in locating the gate leading to the barn. The barn doors were closed but not locked, the interior as Peter remembered it: missing planks and broken panes, loose straw on the floor and a few stacked bales. And the sandbags. Andrew picked one up, tested its weight, and dropped it.

'I wouldn't fancy being coshed with that,' he said.

'I didn't fancy it either,' Peter said. 'You might say it left me speechless.'

'That's quite a feat.' Andrew left the gloom of the barn for the sunshine outside. 'Well, Cathie isn't here. Never was, I'd say. So where now?'

'The farmhouse, of course.'

They returned to the car and drove down the lane to the farm entrance. Peter had not noticed it the previous night, but he was impressed by it now. Fenced with iron railings, a smoothly gravelled drive led long and straight to a cluster of white buildings that seemed to sparkle in the spring sunshine. In a field to the right of the drive horses were grazing. To the left, sheep nibbled ceaselessly at grass already closely cropped.

'Looks prosperous,' Andrew commented.

Peter nodded. He was reminded of the farm adjacent to his school, where the two half-brothers who owned it had lived so bitterly together. They too had kept horses for hire, and it was the horses that could be said to have led, however indirectly, to their tragic deaths.

'Maybe it's crime that keeps it prosperous,' he said.

'Maybe.' Peter frowned as Andrew leaned out to knock the dottle from his pipe by rapping it against the door panel. Andrew ran his finger round the inside of the bowl and put the pipe in his pocket. 'Well, what now?'

'We go in and talk to him.'

'We do? But if he's the man you met in the Close he'll recognise you.'

'So what?'

'He'll know why we're here,' Andrew said.

'True. But he won't admit that he knows.'

'Do we tell him?'

'Of course we don't tell him. We say we're planning a holiday in the district and might want to hire a couple of horses.'

'I don't ride.'

'Oh, come off it, Andrew!' Peter said testily. 'You're being deliberately obtuse. I don't either, but what's that got to do with it? We're only making inquiries. We're not actually going to ride the ruddy things.'

'Sorry,' Andrew said. 'It was meant to be a funny. All right, we inquire. What then?'

'Depends how he reacts. It's my guess he'll play it our way and pretend to treat the inquiry as genuine. But we'll have to see.'

They drove down to the house, a long, low building plentifully bedecked with creepers. Stables and other farm buildings formed separate wings, and from somewhere out of sight came the cackle of hens. Unlike many farms, the whole concept had an aura of order and cleanliness.

Peter stopped the car on the far side of the yard from the house. As they sat surveying it Andrew said, 'You don't think you'd better leave this to me? He doesn't know me.'

'No, I don't,' Peter said firmly. 'If he hasn't actually seen you he'll have had your description, and that fiery fungus of yours is a dead give-away. Besides, if the going should happen to get rough two can handle it better than one.'

Andrew shrugged. 'You're the boss.'

And that, Peter thought, was another reason. It was largely due to his efforts that they had got this far. He had no intention of abdicating now.

Mrs Topping opened the door to them. A tall, angular woman of around forty, dressed in jeans and a blue roll-neck sweater, she had a pleasant face with wrinkles at the corners of her eyes and a deep cleft in a prominent chin. Her blonde hair was pulled tightly back from her forehead and secured with ribbon, although a few wispy strands had escaped to dangle over cheeks and ears. Her husband was busy out back, she told them when Peter gave her the supposed reason for their visit. One of the horses was sick. Would they come back later, or would they prefer to wait? He was unlikely to be long. Ten minutes at the most, she thought.

They elected to wait.

The room into which she ushered them was at the front of the house: a long, low-ceilinged room with a polished floor on which gaily patterned rugs slid as they trod on them. The armchairs were wide and deep and enveloping, easy to sink into but difficult to climb out of. The mahogany furniture gleamed. Two glass-fronted cabinets stood one on either side of the large fireplace, their shelves filled with china and silver and glass.

'Lovely.' From the depths of an

armchair Andrew surveyed the room. 'You know, I've often thought I'd like to be a farmer. Home-grown meat, fresh fruit and veg, your own dairy produce. Lovely.' He sighed. 'Trouble is, I can't abide cows.'

'There don't have to be cows,' Peter said. 'They're not compulsory.'

'I don't like horses either.'

'No? How do you feel about sheep?'

'Indifferent. I can take them or leave them.'

'Taking into account your aversion to exercise and early rising, you're obviously a born farmer,' Peter said.

He had been inspecting the collection of hunting prints that adorned the walls. Now he sat down. Watching him, Andrew saw him frown and press his face against a wing of the chair. He was about to comment when heavy footsteps in the hall alerted them to the arrival of the farmer. They climbed out of the chairs and watched the door expectantly.

Adam Topping was a big man, with iron grey hair and a drooping moustache and an unexpectedly pale complexion that seemed at variance with his occupation. Dressed in hacking jacket and breeches and leggings, he strode purposefully into the room and shook each of them by the hand before motioning them back to their chairs. As he crossed the room to sit by an open bureau, Peter looked at Andrew and shook his head. This was not the man he had seen in Hamble Close.

'My wife tells me you're interested in hiring a couple of horses,' Topping said. 'When would you want them?'

Peter explained that dates were uncertain and that they had yet to fix on a hotel, but that it would probably be for the last fortnight in June. 'This is just a preliminary inquiry,' he said. 'A local garage gave us your name, and as we were passing it seemed a good idea to investigate the possibilities. But we'll let you have the dates as soon as we know. Probably next week.'

Topping nodded. 'The earlier the better. I've only a small stable and the summer's a busy time.' He reached for a ledger. 'May I have your names and addresses?'

Peter gave them. If they had any significance for Topping, in neither demeanour nor tone did he show it. He chatted for a few minutes about the merits of the district as hacking country and then terminated the interview with the information that he had to get back to the vet. 'One of the mares got her near fore entangled in barbed wire, although I'm damned if I know how she managed it. Nothing broken, thank the Lord, but the leg's badly lacerated.' He led them to the open front door, shook hands, expressed a hope that he would be seeing them in the summer, and left them.

They were well down the drive before either of them spoke. Then Andrew said lugubriously, 'Well, that was a frost if ever there was one. Bang on, you said. Was it hell! We didn't even get an outer.'

'Wrong,' Peter said. 'We hit the bull's eye.'

'How? Not with Cathie we didn't.'

Peter turned west out of the gate. 'Would you say Mrs Topping is the type of woman to wear expensive perfume?' he asked.

'Not really. Not that she smelt of cow-dung or anything like that, but — why?'

'Chanel Number Five is expensive.'

'Bloody expensive,' Andrew agreed. 'My Number Two bird suggested I bought her some for Christmas. When I found I'd need an overdraft for even the smallest bottle I settled for bath salts.'

'I smelt it on the chair I was sitting in,' Peter said. 'And Cathie Hackett was wearing it when we dropped her in the King's Road.'

9

Although elated by the discovery that Cathie was being held at the farm, there were certain aspects of the affair that puzzled them. For a start, there was Fillol's behaviour the previous evening. At some time on the journey down from Witney Lane, Fillol must have realised that whoever was following him was looking for Cathie. So why had he deliberately led Peter to the barn? Cathie wasn't there, but she wasn't far away, he had suggested an area to be investigated. If he had doubted his ability to throw Peter off his tail, why hadn't he sought the confrontation earlier? It could be, of course, that it was not until they were nearing the farm, with the Cortina's headlights conspicuous in the deserted lanes, that he became aware he was being followed. Even so, why had he then not travelled some miles further before stopping to tangle with his pursuer? Was he perhaps limited for time in some way? Or was it because the barn had seemed ideal for what he had in mind, and he reckoned that the effect of the assault would be to dissuade Peter from further investigation? In any case, since he could not have seen the barn from the lane at night he must have known it was there. Which suggested that he or his companion or both must know the farm well, that their connection with Adam Topping went further than as accomplices in the kidnapping of Cathie Hackett.

Then there was Topping. Fillol must surely have told him of the incident by the barn and have warned him that there could be further snooping. More than likely Fillol had also been able to give him Peter's name and description — Andrew's too, probably — although it was possible that Topping already knew them. Yet he hadn't batted an eyelid. No doubt his wife's description of their visitors had wised him to their identity and taken the element of surprise from the meeting, but even so, considering that Cathie was actually on the premises, his aplomb had been quite something. And how had Cathie's perfume come to be on an armchair in the Toppings' living-room? It suggested she was a guest, not the prisoner she undoubtedly was.

Despite Peter's reluctance to relinquish control of the situation, when Andrew insisted they now had no alternative but to report their discovery to Hackett he was forced to agree. The next step must be to secure Cathie's release, a task which, short of storming the farm themselves — an adventure that had a certain appeal but which he knew was impractical — could only be undertaken by the police. His hope was that in view of the work he and Andrew had done they would be allowed to take part in the operation — if not actively, then at least as spectators.

Lucy had recovered her good humour by the time they got back to Hamble Close. Too late for the pork, she said; how would omelettes do? Omelettes would do fine, they said, but first they had to talk to Hackett. I heard him come in shortly before you, she said; will you be long? Just a few minutes, Peter said. Then a quick lunch and we're off again.

For once Hackett was alone; Harry had had business to attend to that morning, he told them. They did not go into a detailed account of their investigation. They did not explain how they had managed to identify Daniel Fillol and run him to earth. They made no mention of Lucy, and they did not reveal their knowledge that he had changed his name; he might resent that knowledge. They told him why they believed Cathie was being held prisoner at Warren Farm and they named Daniel Fillol and Adam Topping as two of the kidnappers. They also gave him a description of the man who was probably a third. 'So now it's up to you, Ben,' Andrew concluded. 'You and the police. There can be no danger to Cathie. No one's going to harm her with the police on the doorstep.'

Hackett had listened in silence to what they had to tell him. From the very beginning he had seemed nervous, even jittery; moving restlessly on his feet (he had not invited them to sit), his eyes darting from one speaker to the other as if it were their reactions rather than his own that mattered. Peter wondered if he might have guessed, or at least have feared, that they had discovered he had been born Ben Fillol and not Ben Hackett. Yet why should that disturb him? A change of name was neither illegal nor discreditable, it happened all the time and for a variety of reasons. Gradually, however, his attitude had seemed to change. He was still nervous, but he grew more thoughtful, frowning and pursing his lips as presumably he considered the implications of what they told him. What puzzled Peter was that he displayed little real evidence of relief or delight. It was almost as if he found their news embarrassing, as if he knew he would be expected to act on it and found the prospect of action distasteful or even impractical.

'I'm shattered,' Hackett said, after a rather awkward silence. 'How on earth did you fellows manage it? Where did you start? There seemed absolutely nothing to go on.'

'We just happened to get lucky,' Peter

said. 'Incredibly lucky. But don't let's waste time with that now. Tomorrow's the dead-line, isn't it?'

'Yes. Tomorrow morning.'

'Have you managed to raise the money?' Andrew asked. 'Not that it matters now.'

'Nowhere near,' Hackett said. 'Harry's trying to see what he can do, but whatever it is it won't be enough. I was hoping to persuade them they were demanding the impossible, that they couldn't get blood out of a stone. Now — well, I don't know.'

Andrew was aghast. 'What do you mean, you don't know? Christ, man, it's obvious, isn't it? You don't pay a bloody cent. You get her out. Or the police do.'

Hackett hesitated, scratching the rough skin of his cheek. Then he went over to the cocktail cabinet and produced a bottle and three glasses. Pouring sherry, he said slowly. 'Look, fellows. Don't think I'm ungrateful. I'm not. You've done wonders. But will the police act on it? That's what bothers me.'

'Of course they'll act. Why shouldn't they?'

The police might consider, Hackett said, that the evidence was insufficient. The assumption that the man in the photograph was Fillol could be false, they might say, since only part of his face was visible and the birthmark alone provided no more than a hint of identification; and since Cathie did not appear in the photograph there was nothing to imply that the two were meeting. They might argue that the assault on Peter at the barn did not necessarily mark Fillol and his companion as guilty; even innocent men, understandably apprehensive of the intention of whoever was following them, could have acted similarly. As for the perfume Peter had smelt at the farm — well, Cathie was not the only woman to use Chanel Number 5, and there was nothing else to connect her with the farm except perhaps the rather dubious coincidence of the name. 'Don't get me wrong, though,' Hackett said, sipping sherry. 'Believe me, I'm convinced. But will it convince the police? That's what counts.'

'Of course it will,' Andrew said impatiently. 'It must. And don't forget that Fillol's companion on that trip to the barn was the man Peter saw watching the house two days before Cathie was kidnapped. They can't dismiss that as a coincidence.'

'That's true,' Hackett said.

There was also the fact that Hackett and Daniel Fillol were related, Peter thought. Would Hackett tell them that?

'Andrew's right,' he said curtly. 'Some of the evidence may be circumstantial, but there's too much of it for the police to ignore.' He nodded at the telephone. 'Get on to them right away. Better still, go and see them. We'll come with you.'

'It's a matter for the Sussex police, isn't it?' Hackett said. 'Not the Metropolitan.'

'All right, then,' Andrew said. 'Let's get down there. We don't want to hang about. After our visit this morning they might decide to move her.'

Hackett shook his head. 'I can't go right away. I have to collect Harry at the station.'

Peter stared at him, unable to believe

his ears. What was wrong with the man? Where were his priorities? What did it matter if Harry had to wait, all afternoon if necessary? And weren't there taxis?

'Forget it,' he said, unable to hide his contempt. 'Let him wait. Cathie's more important, isn't she? Or if you like we'll collect him for you. Meet you down there.'

'Thanks, Peter.' Hackett refilled his glass. Peter and Andrew refused. They did not see the occasion as a social one and neither was a sherry drinker. 'But I think not. I'd like to have Harry with me, and a short delay can't make much difference. If they're going to move her they'll have moved her already. Anyway, you fellows have done enough. More than enough. There's no need to involve you further.'

'But dammit, man, there is!' Peter protested. 'The police won't accept hearsay evidence, they'll want it first-hand. From us. Whether we collect Harry or not, we'll have to be there.'

'No.' Hackett spoke with unexpected firmness. 'Not in this case. The Assistant Chief Constable of Sussex happens to be a friend of mine, he won't query the source of the evidence. If he thinks it's enough he'll act. If not' — He shrugged. 'Anyway, there's no need to trouble you.'

'It's no trouble,' Andrew said. 'We're only too glad to help.'

'I know. And believe me, I'm grateful. All the same, I'd rather do this on my own.'

'Selfish bastard!' Andrew grumbled as they went down the stairs. 'We do all the spade-work and he bars us from being in at the kill. I've a good mind to go down there anyway, and to hell with him!'

'He's not just selfish, he's crazy,' Peter said. 'Even if the Assistant Chief Constable were his brother he'd still want to see us before making a decision.' He frowned. 'Or is he crazy? Has he got some devious reason for not wanting us along?'

'Such as what?'

'God knows! He's behaved so oddly throughout that it's impossible to fathom the way his mind works. In fact, if you weren't so sure he loves Cathie I'd say he's not particularly interested in getting her back, that he'll contact the police only because we've more or less pressured him into it.'

'He loves her,' Andrew said firmly. 'No doubt about that. And don't forget he's been raising every cent he can to pay the ransom.'

'We've only his word for that,' Peter said.

Lucy was cross. 'You're late,' she accused. 'A few minutes, you said. Omelettes should be eaten straight from the pan. Yours will be like leather.'

Andrew grinned. 'How about yours?'

'I've had mine,' she said. 'I wasn't going to let it spoil, thank you.'

Despite her prediction the omelettes were delicious. As he swallowed the last mouthful Peter said thoughtfully, with an eye on the door lest Lucy should return from the kitchen, 'We'll have to watch it, Andrew, or that damned woman will be taking us over. She's counting on all this *haute cuisine* to soften our attitudes.'

'Mine's already softened,' Andrew drank beer and sucked at his moustache. 'Think of our meals B.L.'

'B.L.?'

'Before Lucy.'

'Oh! Well, it won't soften mine. She has to go, and the sooner the better.'

'We can't throw her out. She has the drop on us.'

'We can lock her out.'

'We can't. She has a key.'

The telephone rang. 'I've been trying to ring Ben Hackett,' a male voice said when Peter answered. 'But his phone seems to be out of order. All I get is this continuous high-pitched sound.'

'You want to speak to him?' Peter asked.

'Well, no. But he has a friend staying with him. Harry Smith. Would it be possible to talk to him?'

'I'm afraid he's out,' Peter said.

'Really? You're sure?'

'Yes.' Why should the man sound surprised?

'Oh!' A pause. 'How about Ben?'

'Hang on a minute.' Peter went to the window. The Rover had gone. 'He's out too, I'm afraid. Would you care to leave a message?'

'It doesn't matter,' the man said. And rang off.

'What was all that about?' Andrew asked. Peter told him. 'Oh! It couldn't have been one of the kidnappers, could it?'

'I didn't recognise the voice. Anyway, he'd have asked for Ben, not Harry.' Peter bit into an apple and returned to the problem of Lucy. 'She said she intended to stay until Cathie was released. Well, that should be this afternoon. We'll have it out with her when we get back.'

'Back from where?'

'From the farm, of course. You said you wanted to be in at the kill, didn't you? Well, so do I. Come on, let's get going. By now Ben and Harry could be on their way.'

They went first to County Headquarters. No matter what Hackett might have in mind, that was where he and Harry must eventually arrive. That was where the Assistant Chief Constable would have his office; in addition to which no local police station, probably not even a divisional headquarters, would mount such an important operation without first consulting higher authority.

County Headquarters is situated on the eastern side of Lewes, at the end of a turning off the Ringmer road. There was no sign of Hackett's Rover in the crowded car park, and they parked the Cortina in a far corner where it would be concealed from new arrivals. Then, from a convenient vantage point, they watched the entrance and waited for Hackett.

They waited an hour. By then it was clear that either Hackett wasn't coming or he had been delayed, and while Andrew stayed on watch, Peter walked across to the main building. A girl in the large reception hall asked if she could help him, and he explained that he was trying to contact a friend who was visiting the Assistant Chief Constable that afternoon. 'Hackett,' he said. 'Ben Hackett. Can you tell me if he has arrived?'

She consulted the book. 'Has he an appointment?' she asked, shaking her head.

'I doubt it. But it's possible they met away from here. I gather he's a personal friend of the Assistant Chief Constable. Could you check?' The girl looked doubtful. 'Please! It's very important.'

She checked. 'You seem to be mistaken, sir,' she told him, her tone still courteous but slightly less cordial. 'The Assistant Chief Constable knows no one by that name.'

Peter was not surprised. Hackett's claim to the friendship had been invented to bolster his assertion that he could handle the matter unaided.

'Sorry,' he said. 'I must have got it wrong.'

He thanked her and went back to Andrew. Puzzled, they continued to wait. By four-thirty, however, they had had enough. It was clear that Hackett wasn't coming, and it strengthened Peter's suspicion that he was not interested in effecting Cathie's release. Or not with the aid of the police. And what other means was open to him? He and Harry couldn't do it on their own.

'Let's have a look at the farm,' he suggested. 'It's not far out of our way.'

They had a look at the farm. It looked as peaceful as a farm should look. There was no sign of Hackett or Harry, no sign of the police, and certainly no sign of Cathie.

'Do we wait?' Andrew asked.

'No point,' Peter said. 'Let's go home.'

They were angry and disgusted. Angry at having been fooled, at the knowledge that all their spade-work had been for naught; disgusted that Hackett could so readily abandon his wife, exposing her to whatever reprisals the kidnappers had in mind. Had he been going to pay the ransom they would still have been angry, but at least it would have shown a proper concern for Cathie. Yet he wasn't even going to do that. He had admitted that he couldn't raise the money.

'What the devil is he up to?' Andrew asked, after a long, brooding silence.

'I don't know,' Peter said. 'And I don't bloody well care. I've had Hackett.'

'Me too. But I'm worried about Cathie.'

Both men had forgotten the date with Andrew's client until Lucy reminded them on their return. They'll probably give you bits and pieces to sop up the drinks, she told them, but you'll be wanting something more substantial when you get back. Anything special you fancy? She was naturally a cheerful person, and that evening she seemed even more cheerful than usual. Coming on top of the afternoon's fiasco her cheerfulness irritated Peter. He had banked on Cathie's release as a final compelling answer to any argument Lucy might invent for further delaying her departure, and he said curtly that he didn't fancy anything. Disappointment had been less for Andrew, and food was a topic he was always happy to discuss. Make free with the freezer, he said, and surprise us; he had no doubt she would rustle up something extremely appetising. And how about a snack before they left? It was unwise to drink on an empty stomach.

Peter left them discussing what form the snack should take and went out to the conservatory. He was surprised to see two boxes of earth on a shelf at the far end, and wondered momentarily why he had not noticed them before. Then he realised that he had not noticed them because they hadn't been there. Someone had put them there, and that someone could only be Lucy.

'Oh, yes,' she said, when he asked her. 'Andy said you were going to grow tomatoes and cucumbers and such, and you'll need earth for that, won't you? So seeing as I had nothing to do I got some.'

'Where from?'

'From the garden, silly. Where do you think?'

'I thought the garden was just one big jungle,' Andrew said.

'Well, I managed,' Lucy said. 'I couldn't find a spade, so I used a tablespoon.'

'And the boxes?' Peter asked.

'They were in there.' She pointed to the conservatory. 'In a corner. Didn't you know?'

'There's plenty of scope here for a keen gardener. It could keep you busy for months,' Andrew said, and grinned at the almost diabolical look on Peter's face at this hint that her stay might be prolonged. 'What have you done with the *Telegraph*, Lucy? I can't find it?'

'I haven't done anything with it.'

'Well, someone has. It's not here. I've looked everywhere.' He picked up a cushion and threw it down in disgust. Lucy was immediately behind him when he turned, and he thrust his bearded face close to hers in a threatening gesture. 'Are you going to make that double-decker, woman, or do I have to do it myself?'

Lucy laughed and went out to the kitchen. 'That woman's too bloody cheerful,' Peter said gloomily. 'I don't like it. I hope she hasn't forgotten she's sleeping in here tonight. Where's this party, by the way?'

'Esher.'

'What time?'

'Sevenish.' Andrew looked at his watch. 'Leave in about twenty minutes, eh? Mind you, it's not exactly a party. Just a few drinks and a chat. Nothing formal.'

'Suits me.' Peter yawned. 'I feel completely whacked. No energy. I don't think I could cope with a party.'

'Reaction, laddie. You've been dashing around like crazy for the past week. Now it's over and you're left — well, empty.'

'Is it over? Cathie still isn't free.'

'It's over for us.' Andrew looked down at his jeans. 'I suppose I'd better change. These are a bit mucky.'

He was half-way to the door when someone knocked on it; no gentle rap, but an exuberant tattoo. He turned to look at Peter.

'Who the hell's that?'

Peter shrugged. 'Open it and see.'

It was Hackett. But a very different Hackett from the man they had seen a few hours earlier. Clapping Andrew on the shoulder, he pushed past him and strode jauntily into the room. Peter could not recall having seen him smile, but he was smiling now.

'Well, I did it,' Hackett announced. The bold brown and white check of his suit seemed in keeping with his triumphant mood. 'She's free! Cathie's free!'

They stared at him. 'She is?' Andrew said incredulously. 'Honest?'

'She is. I collected her this afternoon.'

It was the word 'collected' that gave Peter what he thought was the clue. 'So you paid the ransom, eh?' he said coldly.

What a waste! he thought. What a bloody, senseless waste! 'Or as much as you could raise. Settled for less, did they?'

Hackett shook his head vigorously. 'I didn't pay a cent,' he said. 'Not a damned cent.'

That floored them. In view of how they had spent the afternoon it was a claim they found difficult to accept.

Andrew said slowly. 'Then how? I mean, we were there. We — '. He stopped. There was nothing to be gained by revealing that they had disregarded Hackett's wishes. 'How, Ben?'

'The police, eh?' Peter said. He couldn't understand how or when, but it had to be the police. 'Your friend at headquarters came up trumps, did he?'

'The police? Oh, no. The police weren't involved.'

'Good God!' The alternative was even harder to accept. 'You mean you actually raided the farm on your own? You and Harry?'

'The farm?' The mystified look on Hackett's face changed to a smile. 'Oh, I see. I'd forgotten you'd told me about the farm. No, not the farm. She'd been there, you were right about that. But they moved her this morning. Had to, I suppose, when they realised you were on to them.'

'So where was she?'

Hackett's smile broadened. 'You'll hardly credit this,' he said. 'But she was on my boat, the *Skye Terrier*.'

10

Hackett was right, they found it hard to credit. Had he claimed to have rescued Cathie from Buckingham Palace their astonishment could scarcely have been greater. Peter tried to rationalise the improbability and found the task beyond him. He said weakly, 'I don't know about you two, but I need a drink.'

'Me too,' Andrew said. He poured three whiskies. Handing one to Hackett he said, 'What the devil was she doing on your boat?'

'And how come you knew she was there?' Peter asked. An unpleasant thought occurred to him and he added sharply, 'Or didn't you?'

If Hackett recognised the implication behind that last question he ignored it. As he was leaving to pick up Harry, he said, he had had a telephone call from one of the kidnappers warning him of what could happen to Cathie if the money was not produced in full the following morning. 'He said someone would contact me early tomorrow with instructions on how it was to be handed over. He also told me to tell you two fellows to keep your noses to yourselves — his expression, not mine — if you wanted to stay mobile. Whether that threatened damage to yourselves or your cars I wouldn't know.' He raised his glass. 'Cheers!'

Mechanically they echoed the toast. 'So what?' Peter asked.

'Well, while he was talking I could hear gulls screeching. I even thought I could hear water splashing against a nearby wall. That foxed me. If Cathie was being held at the farm, where did the sea fit in? I mentioned this to Harry when we met and he got quite excited. When he left this morning he had caught an early train to Chichester — he has a business near there — and had taken a taxi from the station. Along the Southampton road the taxi was overtaken by another car, and he was flabbergasted to see Cathie sitting beside the driver. Or he thought it was Cathie; with the taxi driver blocking his view he couldn't be sure. Then the car turned off towards Bosham and Harry decided he must have been mistaken. But coupled with my telephone call we agreed it was worth investigating. As you know, I wasn't too happy about persuading the police to raid the farm.'

'Bosham is where you keep your boat, is it?' Andrew asked.

'Yes. It seemed a crazy place for the kidnappers to choose, yet I could see that from their point of view it had advantages. Having to move her in a hurry — well, it wouldn't be easy to find an alternative hiding place, would it? They could hardly take her to an hotel. But marooned out in the harbour — and my own boat would be the last place anyone would expect to find her — ' Hackett sipped whisky. 'Well, anyway, there she was.'

'How did you get her off the boat?' Peter asked.

They had left the Rover in the car park, Hackett said, and had walked down to the harbour. Watching the *Skye Terrier*, which was moored well out, they had seen a man leave it in the dinghy and row ashore. Unaware that he was being watched, the man had made for the car park. Harry had followed and had seen him drive away; after which, satisfied that the coast was clear, they had rowed out to the *Skye Terrier*, to find Cathie alone and unharmed.

'How had they treated her?' Andrew asked.

'Well enough. Topping, the man who was with her on the boat — '

'Adam Topping?' Peter said.

'No. Bernard, his brother. He was polite and considerate, she said, but she had the impression he could turn nasty if she crossed him.'

'How about the others?' Andrew asked.

'I don't really know. We haven't talked about it much. My first concern was to get her off the boat and out of the town, and on the drive back she fell asleep on me. Reaction, I suppose. However, there'll be time for talk later.'

'And they're both upstairs, are they?' Peter asked. 'Harry and your wife?'

'No. Neither of them. I dropped Harry

off in Chichester — no point in bringing him back here — and booked Cathie in at a small hotel in Guildford.'

'Why not bring her here?'

'Because I'm aiming to shop Fillol and I don't want her around. I intend to ring him and tell him he can collect the money tonight. He won't know Cathie is free — Topping told her he was meeting his girlfriend and might be late back — and if he agrees I hope to have the police here to meet him.'

'And if he doesn't agree?'

'It'll have to be tomorrow. But I think he will.'

'Jesus!' Andrew exclaimed. 'Look at the time, Peter! We should have left ten minutes ago.'

'You've got a date?' Hackett sounded disappointed.

'Drinks with a client over at Esher,' Andrew said.

'Both of you?'

'Yes. Why? Did you want us to give you a hand with Fillol?'

'No, not that. But Cathie's only got the clothes she was wearing when they snatched her, and I was hoping — I mean, seeing the interest you've taken — '

'You want us to cart some things over to the hotel,' Peter said. 'Is that it?'

'That's what I'd hoped. But if you've other plans — '

'I'm afraid we have,' Andrew said impatiently. 'I'm sorry, Ben, but we need to get a move on. It's a good half-hour's run from here and we still have to change. However, congratulations on the way things have turned out. You must be really chuffed. Tell us about it tomorrow, will you?'

He was making for the door when Peter said, 'Hang on a minute, Andrew. Guildford isn't far from Esher, is it? Why don't we take Cathie's things over to her after the party? It won't last long, will it?'

Andrew shrugged. 'Could do.'

'Really?' Hackett seized on the offer. 'Well, thanks. I'll ring Cathie, shall I, and tell her you're coming?'

'Isn't your phone out of order?' Peter asked.

'Not that I know of. Why?'

Peter told him. Hackett frowned. 'He

didn't say why he wanted Harry?' he asked.

'No. Didn't give a name either.'

'H'm! Well, he was wrong about the phone.'

Hackett departed to pack a suitcase for Cathie. Lucy had stayed out of sight while he was in the flat; but the sandwiches were ready, she told them now, and what time were they thinking of leaving? Ten minutes ago, Andrew said. Rather to their surprise she accepted with equanimity the information that their proposed visit to Guildford would mean they might be late back. In that case she wouldn't bother to prepare a meal, she said cheerfully, they would have to take pot luck. Andrew, impatient to be gone and with his teeth into a handsome double-decker, was for once unconcerned about his next meal. But as he accelerated the Cortina over the ruts of Hamble Avenue, with a thoughtful Peter bouncing beside him and Cathie's suitcase and fur coat on the back seat, the problem returned. 'If we're not too late we might get something to eat at Cathie's hotel,' he said. 'Though I must say I'd like to be back for Ben's showdown with Fillol. I might get some saleable pictures.'

'I doubt it,' Peter said.

'Oh? Why not?'

'Because I don't trust Hackett. I've come to the conclusion that anything he says should be taken with more than a pinch of salt. Preferably a handful. And that includes Cathie's rescue.'

Andrew was so startled that his foot was late on the brake pedal behind slowing traffic. A collision was only fractionally averted.

'Oh, come off it, Peter!' he protested. 'He wouldn't have asked us to take this stuff over to her if she wasn't there.'

'Oh, she's there,' Peter agreed. 'It's his version of how she got there that I doubt.'

'Why?'

In the first place, Peter said, there was the telephone call during which Hackett claimed to have heard gulls screeching and water splashing against a wall. The weather was calm, the water would merely have been licking the wall, not splashing against it; if the call had come from a closed kiosk Hackett wouldn't have heard it. It was doubtful whether he would even have heard the gulls. There was also the mystery surrounding Hackett's telephone. 'If it was out of order, then he couldn't have received any calls and he couldn't have rung Cathie just now.' Peter said. 'If it wasn't, why did Harry's friend say it was?'

Andrew eased the Cortina into the near-side stream of traffic preparatory to turning left. 'Maybe Ben hadn't replaced the receiver properly,' he said.

That had not occurred to Peter. But there was more, he said. According to Hackett, Harry claimed to have seen Cathie in a car near Chichester. Peter thought that most unlikely. If the kidnappers had feared a raid on the farm as a follow-up to his and Andrew's visit they would have moved her the same evening, or early next morning at the latest. But how early could Harry have got to Chichester from Wimbledon by train? 'And another thing,' Peter said. 'If Hackett is so keen to see the kidnappers arrested, why didn't he go to the police in Bosham? They could have nabbed Topping on his return to the boat.'

Andrew had no answer to that. But as they were coming into Esher he said, 'Funny thing. The only part of Ben's story I thought was odd was one you haven't mentioned.'

'What was that?'

'If Bernard Topping was supposed to be guarding Cathie, how come he left her alone for the evening? She could have called for help.'

'True. Well, maybe Cathie can enlighten us.'

★ ★ ★

Peter found Andrew's client pompous and patronising. He had had cause, he told Peter, to remove his son from his present preparatory school and under-stood that Shelton, Peter's school, was reasonably efficient. If Peter could arrange for the boy to be admitted there would be something in it for him. Furious, but mindful of Andrew's inter-ests, Peter disguised his anger as best he could and explained that there was no back entrance to Shelton. If there was a vacancy, and if the headmaster considered the boy to be suitable, he would probably be accepted. Not otherwise.

He was glad to leave. So was Andrew, who had found the situation embarrassing. 'Sorry about that,' Andrew apologised as they took the Guildford road. 'I knew he was a self-opinionated git, but I didn't realise he could be quite so obnoxious.'

'Not your fault,' Peter said. 'Forget it.'

He had not doubted that Cathie would be at the hotel, yet he had become so disillusioned with Hackett that it was a relief to find her there. Yes, she said, Ben had telephoned and she was delighted to see them, and would they mind very much if she popped upstairs for a quick change before they got down to talking? The 'quick change' took over half an hour, during which time Peter and Andrew consumed two pints of bitter apiece and a quantity of peanuts and potato crisps. When eventually she joined them in the bar she wore a red jersey frock, close fitting and short-sleeved and cut low at the back, that showed off her slim figure and long legs to perfection. Peter thought she looked stunning. Judging by the appreciative glances in her direction, so did the other men in the bar.

She drank whisky and ginger ale. Andrew showed her the photograph he had taken in the King's Road, pointing out the elbow they thought was hers. She agreed that it probably was. Studying the photograph further, she jabbed at it with a finger. 'And that's Daniel,' she said.

'Daniel Fillol?' Peter was surprised that she should use the man's Christian name.

'Yes.'

Andrew too was surprised. 'You were on Christian name terms with him, were you?'

'Yes. With all of them after a bit. It was all very friendly, you see. And Daniel is Ben's cousin. Did you know that?'

Peter nodded. 'How did you recognise him?'

'He had an enormous birthmark down the left side of his face.' Cathie grimaced. 'It made me feel sick when I first saw it.'

'What happened when you met?'

Andrew said quickly, 'Hang on a minute. I don't know about you two, but I'm bloody starving. All I've had to eat since lunch is one sandwich and a few crisps. Is it too late to get a meal here?'

'Much too late,' Cathie said. 'I suppose they could rustle up a sandwich.'

'I was thinking of something more substantial. And preferably hot.' Andrew drained his glass and stood up. 'I'll ask the barman.'

Cathie followed him with her eyes. 'I hope he's not bothered on my account,' she said. 'I've eaten.'

'He's not,' Peter said. 'He just has this tremendous *rapprochement* with his stomach.'

Andrew returned with the information that no more meals were being served in the hotel, but that according to the barman there was an excellent fish restaurant little more than a hundred yards away that stayed open until eleven. 'How about it, eh?' he asked. 'Coming? We can talk as well there as here, can't we?'

Peter nodded. He too was hungry,

although he hadn't been prepared to make an issue of it. Cathie said she wasn't eating but would keep them company, and fetched her coat. And for once the distance had been accurately stated. Andrew ordered cod and chips and peas twice, with bread and butter and a double portion of chips for himself, and three cups of coffee. Cheered by the prospect of almost instant food, he said, 'Right! Fire away, Cathie. Get it off your bosom.'

Nothing loth, Cathie obliged. Fillol had told her his wife was anxious to meet her, she said, and they had walked the short distance to his car. Driving south over Battersea Bridge she had reminded him that she had an appointment with her hairdresser in an hour's time. Fillol had made a non-committal reply, and it was only when he had stopped the car in a quiet spot near Tooting Bec Common that she had learned she had been kidnapped.

'He didn't put it as bluntly as that,' Cathie said. 'That's why I didn't scream or anything. He said Ben was in dead trouble, that his freedom and perhaps even his life could be in jeopardy, and was I prepared to help him? Naturally I said I would. But I didn't really believe him. If Ben was in trouble I'd have known. Or I thought I would. Especially if it was as serious as he made out.'

'And was it?' Peter asked. 'He explained, didn't he?'

'Yes.' Cathie hesitated. 'But I'm not sure I should tell you. Ben said I could and I know you're his friends — well, sort of — but it's not very nice. If others got to hear about it — '

'Not from me they won't,' Andrew said promptly.

'Nor me,' Peter said, curiosity overcoming a reluctance to commit himself to the unknown.

Cathie took a deep breath. 'Well, Daniel said the money Ben's been spending all these years isn't his. It's theirs. Daniel's and his friends'.'

'Good Lord!' Andrew exclaimed. 'You mean he stole it from them?'

'Not exactly.' Cathie considered. 'Well, yes. In a way I suppose he did.'

'Who were these friends?' Peter asked.

'The Topping brothers?'

Cathie waited while they were served. The helpings were generous, and Andrew wasted no time. Picking up a fork, he speared a couple of chips and popped them into his mouth. Then he sucked in his breath and his face contorted in pain as he juggled them around with his tongue.

'Jesus!' he gasped, when eventually he managed to swallow. 'Watch it, Peter! They're bloody hot.'

Peter ignored him. 'Who are these friends, Cathie?' he repeated.

'They weren't Ben's friends,' she said. 'Not Daniel's either, really. Just — well, associates, sort of. And not all the Toppings. Only Bernard.'

'Anybody else?'

'Harry Smith.' She smiled wryly at their astonishment. 'Yes, I know Ben pretended he was a friend. But only because he was forced to. Ben hates him. He says Harry is the most evil man he knows.'

Peter shook his head. 'Curiouser and curiouser,' he said. 'Tell us more, Cathie.'

11

According to Daniel Fillol, Cathie said, around ten years ago he had got himself into a complete financial mess; no job, money owing in all directions, behind with the rent and hire purchase commitments, and his wife five months pregnant. Then one evening he had bumped into Harry Smith and Bernard in a pub. He knew Harry slightly, Daniel said, and didn't like him much, but he'd never met Bernard before. Anyway, they got talking, with Harry buying the drinks, and presently Harry asked if he would be prepared to join them in a little job they were setting up. Every Thursday afternoon, Harry said, a wages van collected around a quarter of a million pounds from a city bank and delivered it to the firm's various London branches, calling first at the Whitechapel branch before going south over the river. Normally it kept to the busier thoroughfares, but occasionally, when it was late leaving Whitechapel, it took a short cut down a narrow street carrying little traffic and bordered mostly by large warehouses, many of them disused and in the process of being demolished. 'Daniel says it's different now,' Cathie said. 'Lots of office blocks. But that's where they planned to hold up the van. Dyke Lane, he said it was.'

'Dyke Lane?' Andrew mumbled, his mouth full. 'Now that rings a bell.'

'It's a disease with you,' Peter said. 'Go on, Cathie.'

Daniel had told her he wouldn't have touched it, Cathie said, if he had been sober and not so desperately broke; but the prospect of a small fortune was irresistible and he agreed to join them. For three successive Thursdays they had kept watch on the Whitechapel building, with Harry and Daniel and Bernard in a stolen estate car and a man named Leeson in a stolen Ford van; but on each occasion the wages van had left on time and they hadn't bothered to follow. 'Then Leeson developed appendicitis and they had to find another driver,' Cathie said. 'So they brought in Ben.'

'Why?' Peter asked. He had only pecked at his food. Fish and chips always sounded more appetising than it tasted. 'Why Ben?'

'Well, he was Daniel's cousin. And although he worked in a fireworks factory he raced stock cars as a hobby. And like Daniel and Bernard he was clean. Only Harry had a record.'

'Clean maybe,' Peter said. 'But obviously with a tendency for crime.'

'That's not fair,' Cathie protested. 'He only had to drive the get-away car, he wasn't to be involved in the actual robbery. And they were offering him more money than he could expect to earn in years. Anyone could be tempted.'

'Could, yes. Should, no.'

'Oh, stop moralising,' Andrew said. His plate was empty. He pushed it away and belched contentedly. 'You know something? I remember it now. I *knew* I'd heard the name Fillol before. And Topping. It was just that I couldn't place them.' His cup poised at his lips, he looked at Cathie. 'They got ten years, didn't they? Or was it twelve?'

'I don't know. Daniel said they did eight.'

'Remission for good behaviour,' Andrew said. 'The money was never recovered, was it?'

'No.'

'All right, you remember,' Peter said. 'But I'm still in the dark. Enlighten me, one of you.'

There came a Thursday, Cathie said, when the wages van was half an hour late leaving Whitechapel, and this time the men followed it. When it turned down Dyke Lane the Ford and the estate car swept past. Bernard swung the estate across the front of the van, forcing the driver to tread on his brakes, and Ben stopped the Ford a few yards further on. 'They all wore masks, with Bernard and Daniel carrying staves and Harry a shotgun. Daniel said he and Bernard hadn't approved of the shotgun, but Harry had said it was essential as a threat, although he didn't intend to use it. Anyway, they ordered the men out of the wages van, and when the men refused they blasted open the rear doors.'

'Blasted them open?' Andrew said. 'How?'

Cathie didn't know. But the three of them had carted sackfuls of money to the waiting Ford van, and had been returning for the rest when a coach turned into Dyke Lane from the other end. 'It couldn't get past the estate car,' Cathie went on, 'and when it stopped and the occupants grasped what was happening they came tumbling out of the coach and waded into the three men.' She gave a faint smile. 'Apparently they were members of a Rugby club and far from sober, Daniel said, and if any of them noticed the shotgun it didn't deter them. Daniel and the others tried to escape to the Ford, but before they knew what was happening they were on the ground with husky young men lamming into them with their fists. Daniel said he'd never been so terrified. They had beaten him almost senseless by the time the police arrived.' Cathie paused to finish her coffee. The fact that it was cold did not seem to matter. 'Anyway, Ben was watching the schemozzle from the Ford, and when he realised the others weren't going to make it he got away while he could. Daniel said the police found the Ford where earlier Harry had parked a second get-away car. Ben had transferred the money to it and disappeared.'

'How much money?' Peter asked.

'About a hundred and fifty thousand, Daniel reckoned.'

'And Ben was never caught?'

'No. None of the others grassed — that's the expression, isn't it? — and Daniel thinks that as Harry had a record and was the acknowledged leader of the gang the police concentrated on his known associates first. By the time they got around to Daniel and Bernard, Ben had vanished.'

'To Ipswich?'

'I suppose so. But Ben and I haven't really discussed that. There hasn't been time. Daniel didn't know either. They tried to trace him, of course, when they came out of prison, but it wasn't until last Saturday that they got lucky. Then Dave,

Bernard's younger brother, spotted him at a football match in Wimbledon and followed him back to the Close.' She looked at Peter. 'He got Ben's new name from you, didn't he?'

'Yes.' So that was Dave Topping. 'Sorry.'

'It didn't matter. He'd have got it from someone.'

The men had realised, Cathie said, that Ben was hiding from them as well as from the police. Harry had wanted to use strong-arm tactics but the others had disagreed. The money would long since have been invested, which meant that Ben would not be able to produce it on demand, no matter how severely they roughed him up. They would have to give him time, and during that time he might manage to escape them again. 'It was Daniel who suggested the kidnapping,' Cathie said. 'He reckoned Ben would pay up rather than let me suffer. Harry wasn't so sure. He lacks the finer emotions, Daniel said, so he doesn't expect others to have them. As an extra precaution, Harry said, he would move in with Ben to keep an eye on him.'

'I must say Harry didn't really fit the role of a friend,' Peter said. 'Too damned patronising. I didn't like him.'

'Daniel doesn't like him either,' Cathie said. 'Nor do the Toppings.'

'Nor me,' Andrew said. 'Did you get all this gen from Fillol while you were parked on the common?'

'Most of it, yes.'

'And when did you realise you'd been kidnapped?'

It wasn't a kidnapping in the accepted sense, Cathie said. But Daniel had stressed that Ben must think it was, must believe her to be in danger if the ransom demand wasn't met. They had no fear that he might go to the police, for he would know that even if a police investigation did not reveal his part in the Dyke Lane robbery the men would get their revenge by informing on him. They could do that with no risk to themselves, Daniel had pointed out, as they had already been punished for their part in the crime. 'But he assured me that whether Ben paid up or not I wouldn't be

185

harmed in any way, and that if I promised not to try and escape or get in touch with Ben they would treat me as a guest and not as a prisoner.'

'And you agreed?' Peter asked.

'Of course. I hadn't much choice, had I? It was either that or be locked up somewhere. Besides, I knew Daniel was right. Ben loves me, he would certainly give them the money if he thought I might be in any danger. And that was what I wanted. He'd be safe then, you see, from the police as well as from the men.' Cathie shrugged. 'It meant we'd be broke, of course. I didn't much like the thought of that. You don't, do you, after you've been — well, comfortable? But I'd rather be broke than have Ben maimed or in prison.'

Eyeing the food remaining on Peter's plate, Andrew said, 'Are you going to finish that, Peter?'

'No. I seem to have lost my appetite.'

'Then I move we go back to the hotel. It's more comfortable there, and I could do with a pint.'

Settled in the small lounge of the hotel,

Andrew ordered beer for himself and a whisky for Peter. Cathie refused a drink. She was beginning to look tired, but seemed eager to continue talking, as if it was important that they should know. They had driven down to Warren Farm, she said, where as Fillol had promised she had been treated as a guest. She ate with the family and was not restricted in any way. She had even gone riding with Adam Topping, although only within the farm boundary. 'They were nice,' she said. 'Adam and his wife. If I hadn't been worried about Ben it could have been fun.'

'Did you know we called at the farm this morning?' Peter asked.

Cathie nodded. 'I was reading in the lounge when you arrived. I went upstairs as soon as I heard the car — I always did when they had visitors — but they told me afterwards it was you. That worried them. They knew Ben wouldn't alert the police, but there was the possibility you might do so without consulting him. Bernard was staying there and Daniel came down after they'd rung him, and they had a sort of conference. They wanted to move me, but the question was where? There was no room for me in Bernard's flat, which he shares with a friend — he lives in Aldershot — and Daniel's house would be an obvious target for the police after they'd drawn a blank at the farm. They'd more or less decided to risk it and keep me there when I remembered the boat.'

'Eh?' Andrew spluttered into his beard. 'Are you saying the boat was your idea?'

'Why not? I was as anxious as they were that the police shouldn't find me, and who would think of looking on the boat? And it was only for one night, the money was to be collected tomorrow. They all agreed it was the ideal solution. It was too late to go last night, but Bernard ran me over there first thing this morning.'

'How early was first thing?' Peter asked.

'Crack of dawn. Or it seemed like it. The Toppings supplied us with food and we had brunch on the boat. Later Bernard went off to see his girlfriend. Or one of his girlfriends — I fancy he's got several. This one lives in Southampton.' Cathie smiled. 'He's rather sweet, Bernard. Dishy too. He said he couldn't stay the night at his girlfriend's place — she lives with her parents — and if he drove back to Aldershot or the farm he would have to return the next morning — this morning — to take me home after Ben had handed over the money. So would I be embarrassed if he slept on the boat? Of course I said I wouldn't.' She laughed. 'The poor man will do his nut when he discovers I've gone.'

'You didn't leave him a note?' Andrew said.

'With Ben there? Are you crazy?'

'Ben told us Harry was with him on the boat,' Peter said. 'But he wasn't, was he? Couldn't have been. Not after what you've told us.' He frowned. 'I suppose he thought it would sound odd if Harry had left him to tackle the villains alone. Not exactly friendly behaviour. Did you see him coming?'

'Ben? No, I was asleep. I woke up and there he was. I don't know which of us was the more surprised.'

'Ben shouldn't have been surprised,' Andrew said. 'He more or less expected you to be there. Or that's what he told us.'

She shook her head. It was a rather weary gesture.

'That's what he told me too, after he'd recovered from the shock of seeing me. I knew he was lying because I knew about Harry. Besides, the only one who could have telephoned that warning was Bernard, and he didn't leave the boat until just before Ben arrived. So I explained that Daniel had told me about the robbery, and that although I couldn't say it didn't matter, because of course it did, I loved him and nothing he had done could change that.' Cathie sighed. 'I think the poor dear was relieved that I knew. It saved him having to tell me himself. And he'd have had to sooner or later, wouldn't he? All the same, it took a lot of persuasion to get him to explain how he came to be on the boat.'

'And how did he?' Peter asked.

Ben had known from the start, Cathie said, that there wasn't enough money left to satisfy the kidnappers. It amounted to little more than a third of the sum stolen, and as the brains of the enterprise Harry alone would expect to get most of that. And Harry was tough and mean and carried a gun, and had made it clear that if the money wasn't forthcoming the result for both Ben and Cathie could be extremely painful and, for Ben at least, perhaps even fatal. Ben had believed him, but with Harry parked on the premises and watching him closely he had been given no chance to take action, even had a possible course of action occurred to him. Then, at breakfast that morning, Harry had unexpectedly announced that he had business elsewhere that would occupy him for most of the day, and had left with the warning that the money had better be available when he returned in the evening — or else.

'Did Harry say what the business was?'

'No. But Ben reckons he was planning to double-cross the others — take all the money and disappear with it — and that he needed today to make the necessary arrangements. Travel documents, things like that. It would explain, wouldn't it, why he wanted the money to be ready tonight instead of tomorrow?'

'He took a risk, leaving Ben on his own,' Andrew said. 'But I suppose he hadn't much choice.'

Cathie nodded. 'We think he had finally become convinced that Ben was too concerned for my safety to step out of line.'

'But if Ben didn't expect you to be on the boat, what was he doing there? Skipping, was he?'

'And very sensible too,' Peter said.

'Of course it was sensible.' Cathie's tone was sharp. 'But not the way you mean. He wasn't just thinking of himself, he was thinking of me. He didn't expect them to believe him when he produced only a fraction of the sum they expected and told them that was the lot.'

'No honour among thieves, eh?' Andrew said. Cathie looked daggers, and he grinned sheepishly. 'Sorry, love. No offence.'

Perhaps because it was late and she was tired and wanted to be rid of them,

Cathie let it pass. Ben feared that if the men suspected he was bluffing, she said, they would call his bluff by torturing her and forcing him to listen to her screams over the telephone; and if that didn't work and they had finally accepted that the money just wasn't there, anger would have led them to rough him up so viciously that he could have been maimed for life, if not dead. 'On the other hand, if Ben wasn't there when they came for the money and they couldn't find him, he reckoned I would be safe. They would gain nothing by torturing me, would they, if he didn't know about it? He thought that once they realised they were beaten they would let me go. Anyway, it was a gamble he said he had to take. And he was right, wasn't he?' she ended defiantly.

'Logical, certainly,' Peter agreed. 'Although if he believed he would have only Harry to deal with, who did he suppose would do the torturing?'

'He couldn't be sure, could he? He might have been wrong about Harry. He couldn't take a chance on that.'

'He's taken a chance in returning to the

flat,' Andrew said. 'Did he have the money with him? In cash?'

Most of it, she said. Years ago he had deposited five thousand pounds in a building society in her name. He hadn't touched that. But he had collected the rest from the bank that morning, having earlier in the week asked the manager to make it available. 'He told the manager the truth,' she said. 'That I'd been kidnapped and that he needed the money to pay the ransom.'

'How much?' Peter asked.

'About fifty thousand pounds, Ben said.'

'You had it made,' Andrew said. 'Why didn't you just take off?'

'Ben wanted to. But I didn't fancy being a permanent fugitive. Not just from the men; from the police too. And I didn't feel right about the money. I haven't met Harry, but I like the others. I know they're criminals — ex-criminals, I suppose — and legally they've no right to it. But it's more theirs than Ben's. They went to prison for it, didn't they? I thought they deserved it.'

Peter smiled. 'Not quite the reaction of a law-abiding citizen. The heart ruling the head. But I can see your point. How did Ben feel about it?'

'He took some persuading. But the decision was settled for us. When he checked the engine he found that a vital part had been removed.'

'Bernard being cautious, eh?'

'I suppose so. Although he knew I wouldn't try to escape. Anyway, Ben said there was no hope of getting a replacement this afternoon, it wouldn't be available locally. And tomorrow would have been too late, wouldn't it?'

'So what did you decide?' Andrew asked.

They had decided, she said, to keep the five thousand in the building society and let the men have the rest, hoping that if they could be convinced there was no more in the kitty they would settle for that and not pursue him further. Ben wasn't too hopeful of success, however, so he wasn't risking a confrontation and a possible going over. He intended to ring Fillol, tell him the money was in the flat and where to find the key, and warn him to get there before Harry. He would then book into a hotel for the night and ring her to let her know where to join him on the morrow. 'After that' — she shrugged. 'I suppose we'll go off somewhere. We haven't planned that far. We can't use the *Skye Terrier*; the men are almost certain to be watching it. Ben's going to arrange for it to be sold. We'll need the money.'

Peter nodded. He could believe that. 'Well, I wish you luck,' he said, and meant it as far as Cathie was concerned. 'And now we ought to be going. It's after eleven.'

Since returning to the hotel Cathie had glanced once or twice at the slim gold watch adorning her wrist. Now she looked at it again.

'So it is,' she said. 'Ben should have rung by now. I hope nothing's gone wrong.'

'Such as Harry returning early, eh?' Andrew said. 'That could be nasty.'

Cathie shuddered. 'Oh God, I hope not!'

'Did Harry tell Ben when to expect him back?'

'Yes. Some time after eight. Ben said he should be away long before then. But he reckoned to ring me between nine and ten.'

'He could have rung while we were out.' Peter stood up. 'I'll check.'

He returned with the news that there had been no telephone message. 'Not to worry,' he said. 'Maybe he found difficulty in getting a room. Why didn't he arrange to join you here? Why another hotel?'

Cathie looked embarrassed. 'He — well, he doesn't know either of you very well, does he?' she said. 'Especially you, Peter.'

'What's that got to do with it?'

'Well, he knew I was going to tell you about the robbery — I said I thought you ought to know and he said it didn't matter one way or the other, seeing as he wouldn't be meeting either of you again — and he couldn't be sure how you'd react. You might decide to tell the police, in which case you would also have told them where to find him, wouldn't you? He thought it best to play safe.' She looked from one to the other. 'You won't go to the police, will you?'

Neither was in a hurry to answer. Then Andrew said slowly, 'I don't know, Cathie. It's our duty, really, but — oh, I just don't know.'

'But you promised,' she protested. 'Both of you. You promised.'

'I know,' Peter said. 'But Andrew's right, Cathie, it's our duty. And we couldn't know it was a criminal matter, could we?' He considered. 'Anyway, we won't decide until tomorrow. That will give you and Ben time to disappear. Okay with you, Andrew?'

'Sure.'

'But they'll catch up with him eventually, you know they will,' she pleaded. 'They'll send him to prison.'

'Possibly,' Peter said. 'But after all these years I imagine he'd get a pretty light sentence. It might even be suspended.'

Andrew drained his tankard. 'On your feet, Peter,' he said. 'We don't want to stay until they throw us out. All right, Cathie?'

She nodded without speaking. Nor did she respond to their 'goodnights'. But as they went through the lobby she came hurrying after them, struggling into her coat.

'I'm not staying,' she said. 'I'm coming with you.'

They tried to dissuade her. From what she had told them Ben would long since have left the flat, Peter pointed out. As she didn't know his destination she couldn't contact him, and if she left the hotel he couldn't contact her. He could, she said, she would leave a message to say she had gone back to the flat. She dismissed their reminder that Ben had booked her into the hotel to ensure her safety with the assertion that she would be no less safe at the flat; in the unlikely event that any of the men were still there she would have the two of them to protect her — a remark that caused Andrew to grimace at Peter. Anyway, she said, she had nothing to fear from Daniel or Bernard, and they could surely handle

Harry. It was Ben she was worried for, not herself. If anything had happened to him she wanted to know, and if they wouldn't take her she would hire a taxi. She certainly wasn't staying at the hotel.

They waited impatiently while she collected her belongings and settled her account. Alone on the back seat of the Cortina, with Andrew driving and Peter beside him, she was silent for most of the journey. That suited Peter, whose mind was busy with questions to which he could find no obvious answers. The discrepancy between the reasons given by Cathie and Hackett for the latter's return to the flat needed no explanation. Cathie's account gave the lie to Hackett's. Hackett would never have set a police trap for his former associates, for that must inevitably have resulted in the disclosure of his part in the Dyke Lane robbery. But had it really been to ensure Cathie's safety that he had decided to skip, or was that just a story invented to placate her when he found her on the boat? Wasn't it as likely that it was his own skin he was trying to protect? Was

£50,000 really all that remained from the proceeds of the robbery? If Hackett had invested £150,000 he could have lived very comfortably on the interest without touching the capital. Either he had lied to Cathie about the size of one or both the amounts, or the £50,000 represented all he could raise in a hurry, the balance being tied up in real estate or long term bonds. In which case he and Cathie would not be as broke as Cathie had predicted.

If Hackett had been right in assuming that Harry intended to double-cross Fillol and Topping, then Harry would certainly have needed time to make arrangements. But would he have needed a whole day? Even if he had, would he have advised Hackett when to expect him back? It was as if the warder had given the prisoner a day's freedom in which to do as he pleased. Strange behaviour in a man such as Harry had been depicted. But perhaps most puzzling of all, Peter thought, was why Hackett had asked him and Andrew to deliver Cathie's suitcase to the Guildford hotel. To get them out of the house? They had already told him they were leaving for Esher. If he planned to be away before eight o'clock he could have delivered the suitcase himself and have stayed at the hotel with Cathie. No one then would have known where he was. So that Cathie might tell them the truth? Well, she had. But as she had said, they were not close friends, and only close friends might perhaps be trusted not to pass the information to the police. So why?

Peter gave up.

At that hour of the night traffic was light and they made good time, but it was after midnight when they turned into Hamble Avenue and were alerted by an unfamiliar glow of light in the direction of the Close. 'Something's up!' Andrew said, and started to take the potholes faster.

Watching a plume of smoke climb lazily into the sky, Peter knew that something was very much up. Then, as Andrew swung the car into the Close and braked sharply, he caught his breath.

'Bloody hell!' he exclaimed. 'Look at that!'

12

For a few horrified moments they stayed in the car, with Cathie's blonde head between those of the two men as she craned forward for a better view, and stared over the assembled vehicles and the heads of the crowd at the ruin of Number 3. Little remained of the roof but the smouldering beams. The tall hedge hid most of the ground floor, but the windows of the top flat were gaping holes, the frames and surrounding brickwork charred and blackened. The fire was out, but plumes of smoke drifted upward, to be scattered by the breeze. There was the murmur of voices and the acrid smell of burnt wood.

'Jesus!' Andrew exclaimed. 'What a mess!'

They scrambled from the car and pushed their way through the crowd blocking the road. Cathie kept close behind the two men. 'Where's Ben?' she cried. 'Can you see him? Oh God, let him be all right!'

Beyond the crowd were police cars and an ambulance and two fire engines, the hoses from the fire engines snaking across the ground to vanish from sight in the garden. Police and firemen stood talking, and as Peter emerged from the crowd a constable barred his way.

'Keep back, please,' the constable said.

'But that's our house,' Peter explained. 'We live there.'

The constable eyed them suspiciously. 'You do?'

'Yes. How did it happen, for God's sake? Is anyone hurt?'

The constable ignored the questions. 'Come with me, please.'

Picking their way over the hoses and through pools of water, they followed him to where a uniformed inspector stood talking with a group of reporters. Eyeing the three newcomers, the inspector listened to the constable's report. Then, dismissing the reporters, who moved reluctantly out of earshot, he turned to Peter.

'Your name, please, sir,' he said.

Peter introduced himself and the other two and explained about the flats. There was sympathy on the inspector's face as he looked at Cathie.

'Yours is the top flat, Mrs Hackett?' he asked.

'Yes.' She sounded hoarse. Both hands were tightly clenched. Her elbows were tucked into her sides, as if she needed the pressure to keep herself from shivering. 'Please! My husband! Is he all right?'

'I can't say, I'm afraid.' He paused, lips pursed as if considering. 'Unfortunately there are certainly casualties — two, we think, and both in the top flat — but they have yet to be identified. I hope' — Again he paused. Cathie had moved to clutch Andrew's arm with both hands, her eyes wide with unspoken dread. As if the sight of her grief distressed him the inspector shook his head and turned to Peter. 'May I have a word with you, sir?'

He moved a few paces away, flapping a restraining hand at the eager reporters. A camera flashed. Peter followed, wondering about Lucy. She had known Cathie was safe and had agreed to leave when that happened, so she had probably packed up and gone before the fire started. Was that why she had said they would have to take pot luck? He hadn't seen her in the crowd, and surely she would have come forward if she were there. Anyway, if the casualties were both in the top flat she would not be one of them. Hackett and Harry, he thought, and felt a pang of sadness for Cathie.

'The bodies have not yet been brought out, but I'm told they are very badly burnt,' the inspector said. 'Charred almost beyond recognition, according to the chief fire officer.' Peter shuddered at the image conjured up by the words. 'If one of them is Mrs Hackett's husband it would be best if she didn't see it. Not here, anyway. Not under such distressing conditions. She would be terribly shocked.'

'I agree,' Peter said.

'Do you know Mr Hackett?'

'Yes. Not intimately but — yes, I know him. You want me to identify the body? Is that it?'

'If you wouldn't mind, sir. Unpleasant for you, I'm afraid, but an early identification can be helpful. There is also the other body. Any idea who that might be?'

'I'm afraid not.' He wasn't going to commit himself. Not at that stage. And it didn't have to be Harry, it could be Fillol or Topping. 'Mrs Hackett said her husband was expecting a visitor but she didn't mention his name.' To give Cathie a loophole he added, 'I don't think she knew.'

'His name?' The inspector shook his head. 'The other body is that of a woman, Mr Wilde.'

Peter was shocked. Lucy? he thought again, and again rejected her. It couldn't be Lucy. Yet what other woman would have been in the building?

'How did the fire start, Inspector?' he asked.

That would be determined later, the inspector said. However, according to the occupants of Number 1 the house had gone up like a bomb. Not literally — there had been no sound of an explosion — but it was burning fiercely by the time the fire brigade arrived. 'It seems to have been largely confined to the top floor, which is presumably where it started. But what caused it' — he broke off. 'Ah! They're bringing them out now. Come into the garden sir, will you?' He nodded to a man standing nearby. 'You too, please, Doctor.'

Peter followed the two men through the gateway. The two stretchers had been placed on the path at the foot of the steps, and after a brief word with the firemen the inspector moved to the nearest stretcher and looked at Peter.

'Ready, sir?'

Peter gulped and nodded, and watched as the covering blanket was drawn slowly back to expose the remains of what had once been a face. Now, as the inspector had predicted, it was charred and shrivelled beyond all possible recognition: a mess of blackened flesh and bone, hairless and with no discernible features. Memory of another face flashed into Peter's mind: an old man's face, stained and eroded by nitric acid, that he had seen only a few months' previously. He had vomited then. But this was even more horrible, and he turned away, gritting his teeth against rising nausea.

The inspector waited. Presently he said quietly, 'No, Mr Wilde?' Speechless with disgust, Peter shook his head. 'I'm not surprised. Not much to recognise, is there? But when you're ready I'd like you to look at the rest of the body, and in particular the hands. But take your time, sir. No hurry.'

Peter took his time, waiting for the nausea to pass. When he turned he saw that the face had been covered, leaving only the torso exposed; and although sickened by the stench he found he could look at it without flinching. Perhaps that was because, unlike a face, one torso was much like another, with no features to distinguish it.

The hands were claw-like, little more than talons. They rested on what had once been a stomach, as if the body had been laid out for burial even before death had claimed it. Stooping, the inspector pointed to the left hand. Crouched beside

209

him, Peter nodded. Most of the little finger was missing.

'Yes,' he said. 'That's Hackett.'

Only a few shreds of charred fabric remained to indicate that the body had been clothed, but a fragment had somehow managed to escape the flames. It lay on the stretcher, detached from its garment, and the inspector lifted it carefully and placed it on the palm of his hand for Peter's inspection. Charred at the edges and singed to a light brown, the pattern was still discernible.

'Recognise it?' the inspector asked.

'I'd say it's part of the jacket Hackett was wearing when I last saw him,' Peter said.

'And when was that?'

'Around six-thirty this evening. Mr Liston and I were just leaving to visit one of Mr Liston's clients.'

'Was Mrs Hackett with her husband then?'

'No. We collected her later and brought her home.'

'Oh? Collected her where?'

Although his promise to Cathie was no

longer relevant Peter was reluctant at this stage to disclose his and Andrew's part in the affair, and after a pause for thought he explained that he had known the Hacketts for only a few days, but that as he understood it they had been out together that afternoon and that Hackett had left his wife at a Guildford hotel while he returned to the flat to keep an appointment. 'I believe they were thinking of taking a short holiday. Anyway, when we told him we would be over that way he asked us to leave a suitcase at the hotel; it contained items his wife needed urgently. Well, we did. We also stayed for a meal and a couple of drinks after, and when we left, shortly after eleven o'clock, Mrs Hackett decided to come with us. She was worried that something might have happened to her husband. He had expected to be back well before ten, and there was no reply when she rang the flat.' Peter drew a deep breath. If that wasn't entirely true in implication it was practically true in fact. 'He was probably dead by then, I suppose.'

'So was the telephone,' the inspector said.

His expression suggested that something was puzzling him. Forestalling possible further interrogation, Peter said, 'Didn't you want me to look at the — the other body?'

The inspector nodded. 'If you would, sir.'

The fragment of cloth still lay on his palm. He handed it to a constable for safe keeping. As he moved towards the second stretcher the doctor said, 'Just a minute, Inspector. Look at this!'

Ambulance men had replaced the firemen at the first stretcher, preparatory to removing it. Looking back, Peter saw that the doctor was bending over the body, staring down at the head, which was again uncovered. As the inspector joined him Peter turned away, reluctant to look where he was not required to look. He heard the doctor say, 'There! See that? In my opinion that was caused by a bullet. I think the autopsy will show that the poor devil was shot. Probably dead before the flames got him.'

'I thought he might be,' the inspector said. 'There was a chap burnt to death year before last, over the other side of the manor, and I've never seen anything more horrible. The body was all bent and twisted; incredibly grotesque. One had the impression that he had literally been fighting the flames before they got him. And I mean literally. This one looks more peaceful. What's more, it explains how he managed to get trapped by the flames. I couldn't understand that. But — murder or suicide, eh?'

'That's your problem,' the doctor said.

Peter shuddered. For him that was no problem; Ben Hackett had been murdered. Harry must have returned to the flat while Hackett was still there, perhaps even before Hackett had rung Fillol; and when he refused to hand over the money Harry had killed him and, before leaving, had set fire to the flat in an attempt to destroy evidence that a crime had been committed. The woman's presence, however, was a mystery for which Peter could find no explanation. Nor could he understand why Hackett had been killed.

Wouldn't the threat of the gun have been sufficient? But then perhaps for Harry killing came more easily than threats. He might also have seen it as a tidier solution. A live Hackett could later have become a menace.

Although the woman's body was slightly less charred than the man's the face was equally unrecognisable. More inured now to the sight and smell of burnt flesh, Peter studied it carefully but could see nothing in it to remind him of Lucy. Devoid of hair, it didn't even remind him of a woman. The body was shorter than Lucy's, he thought, but the fire could be responsible for that. Then he saw the rings: three on one hand and two on the other. Lucy's fingers were always generously adorned with rings, but she was not unique in that. He tried to recall her as she had looked that evening, and her hands in particular, but memory was vague. Except that it was something brown he could not even remember what she had been wearing. And although there had almost certainly been rings on her fingers he had no idea how many or on which hand.

'Sorry, Inspector,' he said. 'I can't help you, I'm afraid.'

He was glad to leave the garden. At the gate he had a word with the chief fire officer, who informed him that although the bottom flat had escaped the worst of the fire it was certainly not habitable. Apart from the damage caused by water the ceiling had been holed in several places and was generally suspect. 'I don't suppose the landlord will even consider repairing the place,' he said. 'He'll pull it down and redevelop, and be glad of the opportunity. But if you and your friend need to collect a few personal belongings, clothes and suchlike, go ahead. I'll have one of my chaps go with you, though, to watch that ceiling. If he says to get out you get out quick. And I mean quick.'

Peter nodded. How about the rest of the stuff? he asked. Furniture, for instance. None of it was particularly valuable but they didn't want it nicked. The police would keep a watch on the house, the fire officer said, until such time as it could be made safe for the rest of the contents to be removed.

With a promise to the inspector that he and Andrew would keep the police informed of their whereabouts — it would probably be an hotel until they could find something more permanent — Peter walked across to where Cathie and Andrew stood beside the Hacketts' Rover. He did not relish the task the fire had set him. He had not particularly liked Ben Hackett and he found it difficult to grieve over his death, although he regretted the manner of it. But Cathie had loved him, and he grieved for her.

The expression on Cathie's face as she watched him approach suggested he was bringing news she had already guessed. It expressed hopelessness rather than dread. Her lithe young body looked stiff, tense; he saw Andrew put a comforting hand on hers and guessed that her grip on his arm had tightened. But she did not ask the obvious question — perhaps because she did not want to hear the answer and have suspicion replaced by certainty.

He shook his head. 'I'm sorry, Cathie,'

he said. 'But there's no doubt, I'm afraid. Ben's dead.'

She sagged a little, but there was no sign of tears. 'Yes,' she said softly. 'I know.'

Although probably true, it seemed an odd comment to make.

Two elderly ladies stood close behind Cathie, their faces warm with sympathy. One of them stepped forward and put an arm round Cathie's slim waist.

'You poor dear!' she said. 'How terrible for you!' She looked at Peter. 'We haven't met, Mr Wilde, but I know your name. I'm Isobel Strawan. My sister and I live at Number 5, and we were wondering — well, do you know if Mrs Hackett has any relations or friends nearby that she can go to?'

Peter didn't know. Neither did Andrew. Cathie seemed to resent that the question had been addressed to them rather than to her. Detaching herself from Andrew, she twisted out of Mrs Strawan's encircling arm and said, with only the faintest tremor in her voice, 'You don't have to worry about me. I'll be all right.

I'll find an hotel.'

'You'll do nothing of the sort,' Mrs Strawan said firmly. 'I wouldn't hear of it. My sister and I will put you up. Won't we Dorothy?'

'Of course we will,' Dorothy said.

Cathie looked confused. 'It's very kind of you both,' she said. 'But there's no need to trouble you. I can easily go to an hotel.'

'It's no trouble, dear,' Mrs Strawan assured her. 'We'd love to have you. And it's far too late for an hotel.' She looked from one to the other of the two men. 'That's so, isn't it?'

They agreed that it was.

'That's settled, then,' Mrs Strawan said. 'And we'd be glad to put you two gentlemen up as well if you don't mind sharing a room.'

Both protested that they could not impose on her hospitality to that extent, but Mrs Strawan was insistent. So was her sister. Peter got the impression that a refusal would disappoint them. While he hesitated Andrew said hopefully, 'Well, if you really mean that — '

'Of course we mean it. Now, we'll take Mrs Hackett back and make some tea, and you come along when you're ready. Or perhaps you'd rather have something stronger?'

Peter thanked her and said that tea would be fine. Then he remembered it wouldn't be fine for Andrew. 'You'll have to settle for whisky,' he said, when the women had gone. 'Tough luck.'

Andrew did not answer. Cathie had accompanied Mrs Strawan and her sister without further protest, and he was watching their progress down the Close towards Number 5. Most of the onlookers had by now drifted away; those that remained eyed Cathie curiously but kept a sympathetic distance. A couple of reporters who tried to question her were shooed away imperiously by Mrs Strawan.

'She didn't ask about the other body,' Andrew said. 'I wonder why.'

'Too cut up over Hackett, poor girl,' Peter said. 'Did you know the other was female?'

'No! Was it? Good Lord!' Andrew tugged at his beard. 'Not Lucy, was it?

No, it wouldn't be Lucy. Not if it was upstairs.'

'That's what I thought. Anyway, it was too badly burnt to be recognisable. But there were five rings on her fingers, and Lucy liked her jewellery. I suppose you didn't happen to notice what she was wearing when we left this evening?'

No, Andrew said, he did not. But he wouldn't like to think it was Lucy. She had been a nuisance certainly, but a rather endearing nuisance. However, he agreed with Peter that she had probably gone home. 'I'm more worried about us,' he said. He walked a few paces to the gate to scowl at the ruin of Number 3. Peter went with him. 'The top flat has obviously had it, but what's ours like? That fireman you were talking to — what did he say?'

He was shocked when Peter told him. It could take weeks, perhaps months, to find another flat as suitable and at such a reasonable rent. 'And what the hell do we do in the meantime?' he complained. 'I don't know about you, but I can't afford a hotel. Anyway, what would I do for a dark-room?'

Peter agreed that the prospect was daunting. But already the ambulance and two of the police cars had left, and one of the fire engines was preparing to leave. They should avail themselves of the fire officer's offer, he said, and salvage what they could of their possessions.

Water was responsible for most of the damage, soaking carpets and curtains and bedding and upholstery, but the fire had also taken its toll. Ceilings were blackened and flaking and had been holed in several places, exposing the joists. There were charred holes in the living-room rugs, and burning fragments had set fire to the settee and one of the armchairs. But although the bedrooms had been thoroughly soaked they were comparatively untouched by the fire. Under the watchful eye of a fireman they collected what they considered to be essential, including most of Andrew's equipment from the cellar, and deposited it in their cars. Then, after checking that the doors and boot of Hackett's Rover were locked they collected Cathie's suitcase from the

Cortina and walked across the now almost deserted Close. At the gate of Number 5 Peter halted and put down his suitcase.

'The doctor thinks Hackett was dead before the fire started,' he said. 'Shot. Did I tell you?'

Andrew shook his head. 'No. But I can't say I'm surprised. Harry, eh? Was the woman shot too?'

'The doctor didn't say.'

Andrew was worried. Murder was something else, he said, it was time they talked to the police; he did not intend to fall foul of the Law by withholding vital information. Peter agreed. 'But that's for tomorrow,' he said, 'and before I talk to them I want to get things clear in my own mind. For that I need to hear what Fillol has to say.'

'You're going to visit him?'

'How else?'

'You think he'll co-operate?'

'I'll threaten him with the Law if he doesn't.'

'You can't,' Andrew said. 'He's already served his time.'

'For the robbery, yes. But not for the

kidnapping. He's probably banking on the fact that because it was all nice and friendly Cathie won't press charges. So I'll disillusion him. I'll tell him that Hackett's murder has changed her attitude, that she — we — believe he and Topping were in it with Harry.' Peter shrugged. 'He'll want to convince us he wasn't. So he'll talk.'

'I've got a session in the morning,' Andrew said. 'I might manage the afternoon. Is that too late?'

'Much too late. I want to catch him before he hears about the fire and thinks up some screwy answers.'

'Which means the morning, eh? And early.'

'Very early,' Peter said. 'Such as right now.'

13

It was as well that the early morning streets were practically deserted, for Peter's mind was more on how to handle Fillol than on the traffic. Andrew had said he was crazy, and perhaps he was. The man will be in bed and asleep, Andrew had said, and even if you manage to knock him up he will probably refuse to come down; and the sort of conversation you have in mind can hardly be carried on with him at a bedroom window and you on the doorstep. Peter had agreed that that was true. But talk of the Law should bring him down, he said, particularly if it were shouted from the doorstep. Even if it didn't move Fillol it would surely move his wife. She wouldn't want the neighbours to hear her husband being branded a criminal.

Mrs Strawan had been surprised but sympathetic. If he considered it incumbent on him to break the sad news to poor Mr Hackett's relatives before they heard it on the radio in the morning, that was most considerate of him and did him credit. But was it wise to go driving across London at that hour of the night, and particularly after the shock he had suffered? The hour, Peter assured her, was about the safest time for the journey, and the shock would not affect his driving. Mrs Strawan had not tried further dissuasion. Refreshed by a mug of strong, sweet tea, and equipped with a key to Number 5, he had set off, tired but determined.

He was well on his way when he decided to ring Fillol. Andrew's vision of a doorstep/bedroom-window confrontation niggled him. Despite his rejection of the vision he knew it could happen. But if Fillol could be conditioned beforehand . . .

To Peter's surprise Fillol answered the telephone promptly. Nor did he sound as if he had been summoned from sleep. 'What the hell kept you, Bernie?' he snapped. 'It's after three. What happened?'

Taken aback by this unexpected reception, Peter paused for thought. 'This isn't Bernie,' he said. 'This is Peter Wilde. You know?'

The line went dead. That had been anticipated, and he inserted another coin and waited, confident that Fillol would answer. If he were expecting a call from Bernie he wouldn't take the receiver off the hook, and listening to an insistent brrr-brrr would drive him nuts. Besides, he couldn't be sure that this time it wasn't Bernie.

The ringing tone ceased. 'Bernie?' Fillol said.

'Wilde,' Peter said. 'Listen, Fillol. I — '

'Get stuffed, damn you!' Fillol shouted. And hung up.

Peter tried again. This time Fillol was quicker to answer. Peter didn't wait for him to speak. As the pips ceased he pressed the button and said sharply, 'Hackett's dead, Fillol. Do you hear me? Hackett's dead.'

He heard a sharp intake of breath. 'Dead? How?'

'Murdered. By your friend Harry

Smith. Which means you're in trouble. So listen, damn you, and don't ring off.'

'You're bluffing,' Fillol said, after so long a pause that Peter had begun to wonder whether he was still there. 'He can't be dead. Even if he is it's got damn-all to do with me.'

'It's got everything to do with you,' Peter said. 'You were Harry's accomplice, which means that anything Harry did was done with your blessing. Or that's how the Law will see it when they hear what I have to tell them.' Peter waited a moment before adding, 'Depending, of course, on how I tell it.'

'You putting the black on me?' Fillol said angrily. 'Listen, you — '

'No,' Peter said. 'You listen. I have to talk to you. Tonight. I'm on my way and will be with you in twenty minutes. And I'm not hanging about when I get there. If the door isn't opened promptly I go straight to the police.'

He rang off before Fillol could answer. It seemed to lend weight to his threat.

He wasn't made to wait. But it was Mrs Fillol, clad in what Peter assumed to

227

be her husband's dressing-gown, who opened the door to him. A buxom, attractive-looking woman in her middle forties, she gave Peter a black look and slammed the front door shut behind him.

'He's upstairs,' she snapped. 'You'd best come up.'

He followed her up the stairs. Fillol was sitting up in bed, supported by pillows. Although Peter had seen his birthmark in the photograph he had not appreciated its ugly prominence. It covered practically the whole of the left side of his face, a deep reddish brown in sharp contrast to the general paleness of his skin. A man with a feature so easily discernible, Peter thought, should never have turned to crime.

'All right,' Fillol said harshly. 'So you're here. Now what?' He saw the question in Peter's eyes. 'Broke my bloody foot, didn't I? Dropped a flipping engine on it.'

'Don't expect me to sympathise,' Peter said. 'Not after what happened at Topping's barn Thursday night.'

'You shouldn't bloody well interfere where you don't bloody belong.' Fillol allowed himself the vestige of a smirk at the memory. 'We reckoned to teach you a lesson.' The smirk vanished abruptly. 'What's this about Ben being dead?'

Peter sat down on the only available chair, leaving Mrs Fillol to perch her heavy body on the edge of the bed, and told them about the fire and the doctor's belief that Hackett had been shot. 'And I know all about the Dyke Lane business and its consequences,' he said. 'I also know about the kidnapping and how the three of you planned to collect the money from Hackett later this morning. So don't let's have any bullshit, like pretending I don't know what I'm talking about.'

Fillol had slipped down the bed. His wife rose to help him as he levered himself up, but he waved her away.

'Then what's the big idea, pestering us in the middle of the night?' he said. 'If you know it all what do you want from me?'

'Just a few answers before I talk to the police,' Peter said.

'Look, mate!' Fillol winced as his wife shifted her position. 'I did eight years for that bleeding money, and me and the others had more right to it than what Ben did. All right, so the Law thinks different. But they can't lock me up for trying to get my hands on it, can they? Not again. And like I said, if Ben was killed it wasn't none of my doing. So you can tell the Law what you bloody well please. They can't touch me.'

'They can get you for kidnapping.'

'They can but they won't. And for why? Because Cathie was with us, see? She reckoned we deserved the money. You go telling the Law she was kidnapped and she'll deny it. She was a guest, she'll say.'

Peter shook his head. 'The palsy-walsy bit is over, Fillol. It ended with Ben's death. Maybe you didn't do the actual killing, but he wouldn't have died if the three of you hadn't been hounding him. For all Cathie knows you may even have helped to plan his death. That makes her very bitter. Vengeful, that's how she feels now. And if swearing that she was forcibly kidnapped will put you all away for another long stretch, that's how she'll swear. And no jury would disbelieve her.

You wouldn't have a hope.'

Fillol shrugged, but Peter could see he was worried. So was his wife. 'Why not talk to him, Daniel?' she said. 'Discuss it, like. It can't do any harm, can it? I mean, what more is there to tell?'

Fillol yawned, although whether from genuine tiredness or an exaggerated assumption of boredom Peter could only guess.

'Let's get it over with, then,' he said. 'What do you want to know?'

'Well, for a start, have you been in touch with Harry Smith today? Or yesterday, rather?'

No, Fillol said. During the course of the day he had tried several times to let Harry know of the accident to his foot, but neither Ben nor Harry had answered his ring. 'I got that desperate I even rang you,' Fillol said. 'When you said they was out I didn't know what to think.'

'So that was you, was it?' Peter said. 'Well, it was true. They were both out. Didn't Ben ring you later?'

'Yes. Around seven, it'd be. He said as how he'd collected the money from the bank and to come and get it.'

'How much money?'

'Fifty grand.' Fillol scowled. 'Bloody liar!'

'You thought there should be more?'

'You're dead right I did. A bloody sight more.'

'What else did he say?'

'He said he thought Harry was out to double-cross us. Me and Bernie. He said Harry had told him to have the money ready by eight o'clock tonight — last night — instead of this morning, and he reckoned if we didn't get there before Harry he'd grab the lot and scarper. But he wasn't waiting for us, Ben said. He was going to leave the money there and get the hell out.'

'How were you to get into the flat?'

'He told me where to find the key.'

'But you didn't go?'

'With this foot? How the hell could I? I wanted Bernie to go, but him being on the boat I couldn't get hold of him. I had to sweat it out, wondering if Ben was right about Harry and whether I'd ever see any of the bleeding money. And then

Bernie rings to say Cathie had somehow managed to get off the boat while he was away having it off with his bird!' Fillol swore. 'Bloody idiot!'

'What time was that?'

'About eleven.'

'So what then?'

'Well, I couldn't understand it, could I? I mean, why had Cathie gone? She wanted us to have the money and she knew it was her being kidnapped that'd make Ben stump up. But if Bernie was right and she'd gone, she'd have gone to Ben, wouldn't she? So why was he handing over fifty grand when he didn't have to? Why didn't the pair of them keep the lot and scarper?'

'He wanted to,' Peter said. 'Cathie persuaded him otherwise. She didn't fancy being a permanent fugitive. She also shared this strange notion of yours that you had a right to the money. Or she did until Ben was murdered. What did you arrange with Bernie?'

'I told him to get over to your place and let me know what was happening.' Fillol looked at his watch. 'I'm still waiting, sod him!'

'Tell me about Harry,' Peter said.

Fillol didn't know much about Harry. He had met him only a few times before the robbery and they had served their sentences in different gaols. 'I don't even know where he lives, except that it's New Cross way. All I've got is his telephone number.'

'Does he have a gun?'

'Ben said he did.'

'Would he use it for real, or only as a frightener?'

'How would I know?'

'I'm asking your opinion.'

'For real, then. He's a mean bastard, is Harry. He — '

The telephone by Fillol's bedside interrupted him. He snatched at the receiver. 'Yes,' he said, after listening. 'Yes, I know. Never mind how — what kept you, dammit?' There was another and longer silence. 'All right,' he said. 'Later, after breakfast.' And replaced the receiver.

'Bernie?' Peter asked.

'Yes. He says he got there some time

after midnight. Saw you and the others there, he says.'

'Does he know Ben is dead?'

'He heard people discussing it, he said, but he didn't know for sure. He's been trying to ring Harry since.'

'Any luck?'

'No.'

Peter laughed. 'There wouldn't be, would there? Harry's on his way to whatever haven he's chosen.'

Fillol swore. Then hostility changed to curiosity. 'You sure he killed Ben?'

Peter suspected he was seeking a line of hope to cling to, for if Harry hadn't killed Hackett it was possible there had been no double-cross, that the share-out could still be on. But Peter was not there to spread hope. Proof, he said, would rest with the police, but it was difficult to see any alternative to Harry's guilt. Didn't his decision to move into Hackett's flat suggest that the double-cross had been in his mind from the start? And why else had he brought forward the time for handing over the money without reference to either of his accomplices? 'I expect Ben refused to cough up until you arrived and Harry decided it would be easier to shoot than to grapple. Then he set fire to the flat in the hope that the flames would destroy the evidence.'

Fillol nodded glumly. His wife slid off the bed. 'I'll make some tea, shall I?' she said. She too seemed to have lost some of her hostility. 'I expect we could all do with a cup.'

They watched her leave the room. 'You didn't waste much time, did you?' Peter said. 'Dave Topping spots Ben at a football match on the Saturday and you grab Cathie on the Monday. Quick work.'

'We'd waited ten years for that money,' Fillol said. 'I reckon that's long enough.'

'Not now it isn't,' Peter said. 'Not if Harry's got it. How could you be sure Ben wouldn't answer when you rang asking Cathie to meet you?'

'Bernie was watching the house. He got me on the blower when he saw Ben leave.' Fillol reached for a cigarette and lit it. He did not offer the packet to Peter. 'If there was two bodies brought out of the fire, couldn't the other have been Harry?'

'No way. It was a woman.'

'Ben had a woman with him?' Fillol said sharply. 'Not Lucy, was it? Our Lucy?'

Peter was surprised by the question. He had made no reference to Lucy.

'Why should it be?' he asked.

'She was staying with you, wasn't she? You snatched her.'

'How did you know that?'

Almost condescendingly, Fillol explained. Their meeting with Lucy in the Red Squirrel had not been fortuitous, he said. On his return home that evening he had crossed the road in front of the Herald and had thought to recognise Andrew from a description supplied by Dave Topping. He had mentioned this to his wife and Lucy, and Lucy had said that the car had been there when she left the house before lunch and was still there on her return, although it had changed its position. So later, when the three of them had gone down to the pub for a drink and had seen the Herald in the car park, Lucy had volunteered to go in alone and try to chat up the two men. 'She was doing fine, she said, when she rang to tell me you were giving her a lift home. I said to spin it out as long as she could. I wanted to know what you two were up to.'

She must have telephoned when she went to the loo, Peter thought. 'She told us the two of you didn't get on,' he said. 'Actually, of course, you're as thick as thieves — if you'll forgive the expression. I suppose she gave you a daily progress report from the flat, eh?'

'She did.' Fillol stubbed out his cigarette, grinding it into the ashtray. 'But this woman that was killed in the fire — it wasn't Lucy, was it?'

'I don't know. The body was unrecognisable. But I suppose it's possible.'

'Christ!'

Mrs Fillol returned with the tea. Peter saw the three cups as symptomatic of the changing atmosphere. There was still hostility, but it was more subdued. Perhaps they were beginning to see him as a nuisance rather than as a menace.

Frowning, Fillol watched his wife pour and hand Peter a cup. The action seemed to irritate him. He said harshly, 'If it *was* our Lucy it's you and your mate what's responsible. You took her there. So you'd best think twice about causing trouble, see, or I'll take bloody good care you get done for snatching her. And that's a promise.'

If Lucy were dead he might have difficulty in fulfilling that promise, Peter thought. But he kept the thought to himself. Even the accusation could be embarrassing.

'I'm not out to cause trouble,' he said. 'Not for you, anyway. Any trouble that's coming your way is of your own making. You don't need any help from me.'

'No? Then why the hell are you here?'

'I told you. Some time today I am going to be questioned by the police. I want to ensure I've got the facts right.'

Mrs Fillol had been looking from one speaker to the other, her round face troubled. 'What will happen, Mr Wilde?' she asked. 'To Daniel, I mean. They won't send him back to prison, will they?'

Peter shook his head. 'I'm no legal eagle, Mrs Fillol, but I don't see how they can. Not unless Cathie were to press the kidnapping charge. As I said, right now she's feeling bitter, but I'm sure we can make her see that your husband had nothing to do with Ben's death. And that goes for the Toppings. But your friend Harry Smith — well, he's different.'

'Damned thieving bastard!' Fillol exclaimed angrily, with unconscious irony. 'I'll get him, though. I'll get him. And when I do I'll wring his bleeding neck.'

'I don't know about wringing his neck,' Peter said. It seemed that being robbed of what he saw as his share of the money weighed more heavily with Fillol than the murder of his cousin. 'But if I can help the police to catch him I most certainly will. Thanks to Harry, Andrew and I are now homeless.' He sipped his tea and looked at the woman. 'I suppose you don't happen to know if Lucy got home all right tonight?'

'Tonight?' Mrs Fillol tucked in her chin in a gesture of surprise. 'I thought she wasn't coming back till tomorrow. That's what she said.'

'Oh? When was that?'

'This afternoon.' She turned to her husband. 'She rang just after tea, Daniel. You were asleep and she said not to wake you; it wasn't important, she said.' She gave Peter a quick, almost apologetic glance. 'She said Mr Wilde and his friend were going to a party this evening and she'd ring later.'

'But she didn't, did she?' Fillol said.

'No. Why?' She saw the look on their faces. 'She's all right, isn't she? Nothing's happened?'

'It's possible, love. There was a woman died in the fire. They found her body in Ben's flat. We think it may have been Lucy.'

'Oh, no! Oh, how dreadful! Poor Lucy.'

She fumbled for a handkerchief in the pockets of the dressing-gown. Then, muttering something Peter did not catch, she hurried from the room.

'She's properly cut up,' Fillol said. 'She was fond of Lucy.'

'I'm sorry,' Peter said. 'But can you think of any reason why Lucy should have gone up to Ben's flat? While she was with us she took good care to avoid him.'

'You couldn't never tell what Lucy would do,' Fillol said. 'Unpredictable, that was Lucy. But if you ask me I'd say she just got curious. Wanted to see how much he'd changed. After all, it's been ten years.'

'Changed? They knew each other before, did they?'

'Of course they knew each other,' Fillol said. 'She was his wife, wasn't she?'

14

A sudden bump on the bed woke him. It was a reluctant awakening. His eyelids seemed to be glued down and he had to rub them to free them. As his eyes opened they were assailed by light, and he shut them quickly and turned away, pulling at the bedclothes to cover his head.

'Get up, you lazy bastard,' Andrew said.

For a few moments he lay still. Then his brain became active and he knew he had to get up, there were things to do. He knew too that even if the day ahead were devoid of all commitments he would still have to get up. Andrew would see to that.

'What time is it?' he asked, his head still under the bedclothes.

'Quarter to ten. What time did you get in?'

'God knows! Just before you woke me, I think.'

He pulled down the covers and cautiously opened his eyes again. Andrew sat on the bed, dressed in jeans and a stained sweater and with traces of egg on his beard. Peter stretched and yawned. Dawn was just breaking when eventually he had crawled into bed, but he had found sleep difficult to achieve. His head ached, his limbs felt stiff, his eyes were hot and the lids heavy; his brain refused to stop working. When he had succeeded in shutting out one of the day's many dramas another took its place. But it was the fire and its aftermath that had stayed with him the longest. In imagination he had even seen the flames and two demented creatures writhing and screaming as the fire engulfed and destroyed them. And Lucy. According to Fillol, Lucy and Hackett had never been divorced; if she were dead, as now seemed certain, they had died together as man and wife. Had Hackett and Cathie gone through a bigamous marriage? If so, had Cathie known it was bigamous? Or had the two of them simply lived together without the ceremony? In any case she wasn't a widow.

He could not remember when sleep

had finally come, but he wished it had come sooner. He had a lot to catch up on.

'I see you've had breakfast,' he said. 'One egg or two?'

'Three. And if you don't want to go hungry you'd best get a move on. The old dears can't be expected to keep breakfast going indefinitely.'

'Is Cathie up?'

'No. They gave her breakfast in bed.'

'Any sign of the police?'

'Not here. There's been some activity at Number 3.'

Dressing, Peter related what he had learned from Fillol. Andrew had had a certain regard for Lucy — her culinary skill had brought a new dimension to meals in the flat and, unlike Peter, he had not been robbed of his bed — and the apparent finality of her fate distressed him. 'But why make out she was a widow?' he said. 'I can see why she wouldn't want us to know that Ben was her husband. But why a widow? Why not simply say that she and her husband were separated?'

'I can guess,' Peter said. 'She gave her

245

correct name in the pub because she wanted us to assume she was Daniel's wife. When we discovered she wasn't — well, whose wife was she? Fillol's an uncommon name, he was more than likely to be a relative. So she would reason that if we knew Ben's surname had originally been Fillol, as we might, and she told us she and her husband were separated, we might put two and two together and come up with four. So she played safe.' Peter frowned. 'We were a bit dim, though, weren't we? Why did we so readily accept that she was a widow?'

Andrew shrugged. 'Does it matter? But I wonder what induced her to visit Ben?'

'Feminine curiosity, according to Fillol. But I suspect there was more to it than that. She knew the money was to be handed over this morning, which meant he must already have collected it from the bank. I think she decided that some of it should come to her. After all, he was more than ten years behind with the housekeeping, so to speak. She'd never had a penny from him after he walked out.'

'That bastard Harry!' Andrew said, with uncustomary venom. 'I liked Lucy. I really liked her.'

'So did I,' Peter said. 'Not in the flat, perhaps, but as a person. But Harry' — He shrugged. 'If he found them together — well, it had to be both or neither. He couldn't leave a witness.'

Andrew remembered he had a client to meet and the prospect of a session that would occupy the morning and might extend into the afternoon. So it was up to Peter to find them somewhere to sleep, he said. They might possibly impose on Mrs Strawan's hospitality for one more night, but after that they were homeless. 'And how about getting busy with the estate agents?' he said. 'You know the sort of place we want.'

'Anything else?' Peter said. 'I wouldn't want to be idle.'

Andrew grinned. 'I'll let you know. Oh, about Cathie. I gather we don't let on that we know she and Ben weren't married. Right?'

'Right.'

Peter found Cathie in the breakfast

room. She stood at the window, staring across the Close at the ruin of Number 3. When he entered she turned and gave him a faint smile.

'How did you sleep?' he asked.

'Better than I expected,' she said. 'And you?'

'Like a log when I eventually got down to it.'

She did not query the 'eventually'. He had not told her of his intention to visit Daniel Fillol, and as she made no reference to it now he assumed no one else had mentioned it either. Or perhaps she was still too shocked by Hackett's death to be interested.

Mrs Strawan brought him breakfast. With Cathie present she made no direct reference to the previous night's tragedy or to his subsequent nocturnal expedition, and Peter approved her tact. She had told Mrs Hackett, she said, that she was welcome to stay for as long as it took to make other arrangements, and the same went for himself and Mr Liston. Nor were they to think that they would be an encumbrance, because the pleasure

248

would be hers. And her sister's, of course. With her children and grandchildren domiciled abroad, visitors to Number 5 were few. Much as she deplored the tragedy that had resulted in the three of them being her guests, she was delighted to have them.

The warmth and sincerity of the invitation embarrassed Peter. It seemed churlish to refuse, parasitic to accept. Yet acceptance would put a strain on his and Andrew's freedom of movement, and he thanked her as graciously as he knew how and explained that, with the special requirements that Andrew's occupation demanded, finding a suitable flat might take weeks, perhaps months. They couldn't impose on her that long. So, as they had to move, it would be best to go sooner than later, before her generous hospitality sapped their will to leave. 'Temporary accommodation shouldn't be hard to find,' he said. 'The holiday influx hasn't really started, has it?'

She did not press him further. She chatted for a while, then left him to finish his breakfast. Cathie came to the table, poured herself a cup of coffee, and sat facing him. Staring, she said, 'I heard Andrew talking to Mrs Strawan about the fire. He said the other person killed was a woman. Is that true?'

Damn Andrew's big mouth! he thought. 'Yes,' he said.

'Do you know who?'

He knew she was troubled that Ben might have had another woman. Well, at least he could put her mind at rest on that. 'I think so,' he said. 'I'm not sure, but I think it was someone who was spending the night in our flat.' That sounded bad, and he added hastily. 'An elderly lady.'

'I'm sorry,' she said.

'We didn't really know her,' he said. 'A friend asked us to give her a bed for the night.'

It sounded implausible but she did not comment. 'Why would she have gone up to our flat?' she asked.

'That's something we'll never know, I'm afraid.'

'I suppose not.'

Buttering toast, he said. 'The police

could be here at any moment, Cathie. Have you decided what you're going to tell them?'

She stared at him wide-eyed. 'The truth, of course.'

'All of it? Including Ben's part in the Dyke Lane affair?'

'I suppose so.' She sighed. 'It can't hurt Ben now, poor darling. Why? Do you think I shouldn't?'

'I think you should. Although I hope you'll go easy on the kidnapping lark. Otherwise Fillol and Bernard Topping are likely to land up back in gaol. You don't want that, do you?'

'Of course not. I'll say I stayed with them of my own free will. Which I did.'

'Good.' He finished his coffee and stood up. 'Well, I've things to do. Are you accepting Mrs Strawan's invitation to stay on here?'

'Perhaps. I don't know. My mother's away on holiday, or I'd go to her.'

As he went upstairs to his room he reflected that they never had learned where her mother lived.

The police arrived as he was leaving: a

251

Superintendent Greenhough and the inspector of the previous night. They met at the door, and the inspector explained that they wished to question him and the other former occupants of Number 3, and would he be good enough to wait until they had spoken with Mrs Hackett? The inspector's manner was polite; but perhaps because of a guilty knowledge that he had not been entirely frank the previous evening Peter thought to detect a certain coolness in his tone. That riled him. Mr Liston had left, he said. As for waiting, the police should appreciate that the two of them were now homeless, and that unless he got cracking on his quest for other accommodation they could well be sleeping rough. A short delay would not make much difference, the inspector said, and if the worst came to the worst there was always the local nick. The cells might not be sumptuous but they were scrupulously clean. So would he please wait?

Peter relented. Put like that, he said, he would be churlish to refuse.

He sat in the hall and scanned the

advertisement pages in the *Daily Tele-graph*. Listening to the murmur of voices from the room where Cathie was being interrogated he was reminded of the first occasion on which he had been inter-viewed for a teaching job. Waiting then while the headmaster interviewed another applicant he had wondered how his rival was coping. Now he wondered about Cathie. She had said she would conceal nothing. If she stuck to that it would make his own interrogation easier.

When Cathie came out he thought she looked strained, as if she had been through a difficult and tiring ordeal; but with the inspector beckoning him from the doorway he was given no opportunity to question her. And now it was Superintendent Greenhough who did the talking. As Peter must be aware, he said, two people had died in circumstances which suggested the possibility of homicide, and from what Mrs Hackett had told them it seemed likely that he was in possession of information which could help the police in their inquiries. 'It's a nasty business, Mr Wilde,' the superintendent concluded. 'And apparently far from straightforward. Lots of loose ends. We would appreciate your co-operation.'

'I know nothing about last night,' Peter said. 'I was out. So was Andrew — Mr Liston. By the time we got back it was all over.'

'I wasn't referring to last night,' the superintendent said. 'Or not specifically. It's your activities during the past week that interest me. Suppose you tell us about them?'

Peter told them — from his meeting with Dave Topping on his arrival in the Close to his and Andrew's visit to Cathie at the Guildford hotel. But when he started to repeat what Cathie had told them the superintendent stopped him.

'We've had all that from Mrs Hackett,' the superintendent said. 'No need to go through it again.' He turned to the inspector. 'Any comment?'

The inspector looked at Peter. 'Mr Wilde's memory seems to be in better shape this morning than it was last night,' he said.

'All right,' Peter said, irritation returning. 'But when one arrives home in the small hours to find the place in flames and two people dead, somehow one's appetite for largely irrelevant detail tends to flag. And if I didn't give you the whole truth, Inspector, to the best of my recollection I gave you nothing but the truth.'

The inspector shrugged. 'With certain euphemisms, sir.'

'Yes. Well, we'll leave that, shall we?' the superintendent said smoothly. 'About the two bodies found in the fire, Mr Wilde. You identified one as being that of Benedict Hackett?'

'Yes.' Odd, Peter thought. I assumed his name was Benjamin.

'Based on a missing finger and the pattern of his jacket, eh?'

'Yes.'

'We shall, of course, require a more positive form of identification.' The superintendent sipped water. 'You couldn't identify the woman?'

'I could have made a guess, but I decided that might be misleading.'

'It might have been helpful,' the inspector said. 'We could have checked it out.'

Peter shrugged.

'So what is your guess?' the superintendent asked. 'Mrs Fillol? The woman you kidnapped?'

'If you put it like that — yes.'

'I do put it like that, Mr Wilde.'

'She could have left whenever she chose,' Peter argued. 'We *wanted* her to leave. Unfortunately she preferred to stay.'

'Nevertheless she was kidnapped. Your intention may have been good, but kidnapping is a serious crime. You must know that.'

Peter nodded. He did know it. The knowledge did not worry him — how could they charge him without Lucy to substantiate the charge? — but he continued to feel guilty about her death. It could not have happened had he not brought her to the house. That she had later acted of her own volition could not alter that.

To distract their attention from the

kidnapping he told them of his visit to Lewisham and his early morning talk with the Fillols, although he gave it a more amicable flavour than it had in fact possessed. Nor did he mention that Cathie had never been married to Hackett. Either Cathie had told them and they already knew, or they would learn it from Fillol when they questioned him, as obviously they must. He preferred that they should not learn it from him.

The interview concluded with a request from the superintendent (he made it sound like an order, and Peter interpreted it as such) that Peter should inform the local nick of his address when he eventually settled on one. 'And ask Mr Liston to contact us at his earliest possible convenience, please.' The superintendent stood up and stretched. 'Later we shall want you to sign a formal statement. All right?'

'All right,' Peter said.

'Yes.' The superintendent hesitated. 'You've been sailing in pretty muddy waters, Mr Wilde, and mud sometimes sticks. So let me give you a word of advice. See a solicitor and tell him what you have just told us.'

'You think that's necessary?'

'I think it would be a very wise precaution,' the superintendent said.

It might be a precaution, but Peter considered it less urgent than the need to find accommodation and he dismissed it temporarily from his mind. He half expected to find reporters waiting when he left; but no one accosted him, no cameras were levelled, and he realised that the fire had not been sufficiently important to warrant heavy Press coverage. Even the fact that two people had died had earned only a column inch in the *Telegraph*. No doubt greater interest would have been aroused had the drama behind the deaths been made public. But that was information the police were as yet not prepared to release.

His search for accommodation was less protracted than he had feared. The few small hotels he visited in Wimbledon were either full or unsuitable, and he moved on to Richmond. There he struck lucky, at a guest house newly opened by a young couple named Kendrick. The Kendricks had heard of the fire and were sympathetic. They had two adjacent rooms vacant on the first floor, they said. Only one was furnished; but they could put a camp bed and a chair and some form of wardrobe in the other, and if Peter or his friend was prepared to make do with that until proper bedroom furniture could be bought and installed they were welcome to move in right away. Peter suspected they were short on capital and suggested using some of the undamaged furniture from the flat. The Kendricks accepted the suggestion with alacrity. Bring the lot, they said, what you don't need can be stored in our shed. Peter was delighted; the offer solved two problems where he had sought to solve only one. The terms quoted were only slightly higher than those he and Andrew had agreed would be acceptable, and he did not hesitate. Put up the camp bed, he said, we'll be moving in this evening.

Lack of sleep had caught up with him by the time he returned to Number 5, and he went up to the room he had shared with Andrew and slept for a couple of hours. Then he packed his and Andrew's suitcases and took them down to the Triumph. In the daylight the ruin of Number 3 looked even blacker and more stark than at night. A constable stood near the gate, and Peter was surprised to see two men leave the house and come down the steps. He went across and introduced himself. One of the men was the landlord's agent. Peter asked if he knew when it would be safe for them to move their belongings. The ground floor's safe now if you watch it, the man said, or we wouldn't be nosing around. And ask Mr Liston to look in at the office, will you? There are certain matters to be settled.

Mrs Strawan insisted on giving him tea before he left. 'I'm glad you've found somewhere nice,' she said, busy with a silver teapot. 'I just hope poor Mrs Hackett has been as lucky. So sad, losing her husband like that.'

'She's young,' her sister said, as if youth lessened the impact of tragedy.

Through the window Peter saw the

agent and his companion drive away, leaving the area outside Number 3 devoid of cars. So where was Hackett's Rover? Strange he hadn't noticed earlier that it had gone.

'Has Mrs Hackett left?' he asked.

Mrs Strawan nodded. 'She went after lunch.'

'In the Rover? Her husband's car?'

'Yes. Apparently she had a spare set of keys.' Mrs Strawan pointed to the cake stand. 'Try one of these, Mr Wilde. Not home made, I'm afraid, but they're usually quite good.'

Peter took one. He was puzzled. At breakfast Cathie had been undecided. 'Did she say where she was going?' he asked.

'Unfortunately no.'

'Unfortunately?'

'She forgot her vanity case,' Dorothy explained.

'Oh! Well, if we knew where she was I might have taken it over to her,' Peter said. 'I've a couple of hours to kill before meeting Andrew. However, I expect she'll be in touch.'

Dorothy got up and left the room, to return with a crumpled slip of paper which she handed to Peter. 'I think that's the telephone number,' she said.

'However do you know that, Dorothy?' Mrs Strawan said sharply.

Her sister explained. She had been on her way upstairs to rest after lunch when Cathie had asked to use the telephone, and from the landing she had seen Cathie take a piece of paper from her handbag, dial a number, and then crumple the paper and drop it in the wastepaper basket. 'I didn't listen to her conversation, of course,' Dorothy said. 'But you could try the number, couldn't you?'

'Yes.' 01 indicated a London number. '723. What code is that? Do you know?'

'Paddington,' Mrs Strawan said promptly. 'My brother has a flat there.'

'Fine,' Peter said. 'I'll give her a ring.'

The voice that answered his call was young and feminine but not Cathie's. 'The Ashleigh Arms,' the voice said. 'Can I help you?'

So Cathie had gone to an hotel. 'I'd

like to speak to Mrs Hackett, please,' Peter told her.

'One moment, please.' There was a pause while she consulted the register. 'I'm sorry, sir. There is no one of that name staying here.'

'Maybe she hasn't arrived yet,' Peter said. 'But I believe she booked a room shortly after lunch this afternoon.'

Another pause. 'You must be mistaken, sir,' the girl said. 'We've had no bookings this afternoon. The last was at eleven o'clock this morning.'

Dorothy thought she had the answer to the mystery. 'If she wasn't booking a room she must have wanted to talk to someone staying in the hotel, mustn't she?' Dorothy said. 'Perhaps she was arranging a meeting there.'

Peter agreed she could be right. 'I'll drive over there, anyway,' he said. 'I'd like to see her, find out what she's doing. If she has left before I get there — well, I expect I can find out who she was meeting and learn where she's gone. I've one or two chores to do first, but I'll still have time to kill.'

'Will you take the vanity case?' Mrs Strawan asked.

'I may as well. If I don't catch up with her I'll bring it back tomorrow. I have to arrange for our furniture to be collected.'

The 'one or two chores' were to stop the milk and newspaper deliveries to the flat and to settle outstanding bills. That done, he checked the Ashleigh Arms with the RAC handbook, to discover that it was listed as a two-star hotel with nine bedrooms. The figure of nine bedrooms was encouraging, there would be only a small number of guests to question. How to question them he wasn't sure. Did he go round knocking on doors? Anyone here seen Cathie? Perhaps not. He would probably have to rely on the receptionist.

When he drove into the car park of the Ashleigh Arms he was delighted to see Hackett's Rover there and to know that his journey had not been wasted. But Cathie wasn't in the hotel lounge and the bar and the dining-room were closed, and he sought out the receptionist. 'I'm the fellow who rang earlier,' he told her, his eyes brightening. She was a very pretty girl. 'I was inquiring after a Mrs Hackett. Remember?'

'I remember,' she said. 'But didn't I tell you she isn't staying here?'

'You did. But as I was in the neighbourhood I decided to look in on the off chance. She might have arrived later. And it seems she did. Her car's in the car park.'

'It is?' She frowned, nibbling at a pencil. Then she brightened. 'The gentleman in Number 7 had a visitor this afternoon. I saw them together in the lounge. A blonde lady. Could that be her?'

'It could,' Peter said. 'But she's not in the lounge now. I looked.'

'Perhaps they went out. Or they could have gone up to his room.'

'I'll check,' Peter said. 'Where's Number 7?'

'Up the stairs, turn left, and it's at the end of the corridor. You can't miss it.'

He didn't miss it. Outside the room he stood listening for voices, and heard none. When eventually he knocked the door was opened almost immediately, and

Cathie confronted him. He was not surprised that she should be startled by his unexpected appearance. But she was also strangely concerned, for she did not move aside for him to enter but stood with one arm outstretched as if barring his way.

'Surprise, surprise, eh?' Gently he pushed her arm down and went in, curious to see the man she was visiting. But Cathie was alone, and he walked round the twin beds to the dressing-table. 'You weren't all that difficult to find. Anyway, you left your vanity case at Mrs Strawan's and she asked me — '

He broke off. The dressing-table was at the opposite end of the room to the bathroom. Now the bathroom door had opened, and standing in the doorway and reflected in the mirror was the tall figure of Ben Hackett.

15

'Unfortunate,' Hackett said. 'Most unfortunate. For all of us.'

He sat on the edge of the bed furthest from Peter, nude from the waist up and holding a shiny black automatic which he had produced from under the pillow. Cathie was behind him, leaning against the closed bathroom door. They both watched Peter, waiting to see what he would do. But Peter was too startled to do anything. He stared back at them, striving to adjust to the situation.

Hackett placed the gun on the bed. 'Bit of a shock, eh?' he said. 'Yes, I suppose it would be.'

Peter nodded. He felt a need to sit down. There was a chair a few paces away, but as he made a move towards it Hackett's hand reached for the gun and then drew back.

'I thought' — Peter swallowed, clearing the constriction in his throat. 'We all thought you were dead.'

'That's what you were supposed to think,' Hackett said. 'Except Cathie, of course. Cathie knew it was Harry.'

That was another shock. Peter looked at Cathie, who gave him an uncertain smile. 'But you seemed so distressed,' he said. 'Last night — this morning — it couldn't just have been an act.'

'Cathie used to be an actress,' Hackett said. 'A good actress too, although she never got a big enough part to prove it. But you're right about her being distressed. She was. She wasn't expecting the woman, you see. Didn't know what to make of it. That upset her.'

'Lucy?' Peter said.

'Yes.'

'You killed her?'

'I had to. Otherwise the whole scheme would have fallen apart.' Without turning, Hackett put out a hand. Cathie took it and squeezed it. 'Cathie was horrified when I told her. It still upsets her to think of it, but she understands. Or I hope she does. It upsets me too; killing isn't my scene. But I was committed, you see.'

'No,' Peter said. 'I don't.' Despite the gun he felt no fear. Hackett wouldn't dare to use it; not in a hotel bedroom. Quite how the situation would be resolved he had no idea, but it wouldn't be by force. 'I suppose you wouldn't care to explain?'

Hackett pursed his lips, considering. Then, somewhat to Peter's surprise, he nodded.

'I don't see why not. None of us is going anywhere. Not yet, anyway. Not until we've sorted this out. You want to sit down?' Peter nodded. 'Okay, go ahead. And pour us all a drink, Cathie, eh?' He pointed to a tray on which stood a bottle of whisky and two glasses. 'You can give me the toothmug.'

Neither Daniel Fillol nor Bernard Topping had had a reputation for violence in the past, Hackett said, but that did not lessen his fears for Cathie's safety when he learned that she had been kidnapped. After eight years in gaol and months of looking for him they would be desperate to get their hands on the money, and with their anger against him for having tried to bilk them he suspected they would not shirk from using desperate methods to get it. But it was Harry Smith's constant presence and Harry Smith's reputation that really put the pressure on him. 'He was a real mean bastard,' Hackett said, smiling at Cathie as she handed him the mug. 'Like I said, killing isn't my scene. But somehow I couldn't feel bad about Harry. Just glad he wasn't there to torment me any more.'

'You were about his size and weight,' Peter said. 'Did you have to kill him? Couldn't you have tackled him physically?'

'You kidding? He had a gun, didn't he?'

'Ah!' Peter sipped whisky. 'I'd forgotten the gun.'

'He didn't let me forget it,' Hackett said. 'Kept it in his jacket pocket and was always flashing it around. Once — to show it wasn't a toy, he said — he actually used it. Missed me by inches.'

'So when did you kill him?'

'Friday morning. He woke up with diarrhoea, and in the middle of breakfast he had to make a dash for the loo. Left his jacket on the back of the chair, with the gun in the pocket. So I lifted it, and when he returned I told him I was going to hang on to it and if he didn't bloody well behave himself I just might use it. Mind you, I wasn't trying to wriggle out of the deal; not with them still holding Cathie. I told him so, too. But he lost his temper and came at me, and almost without realising what I was doing I pulled the trigger and — wham! Down he went.' Hackett shook his head. 'Funny thing, that. First time I'd used a gun and I get a bull's eye. Drilled him bang in the middle of his forehead.'

'I know,' Peter said.

Aware that if Fillol or Topping rang they would expect to speak to Harry, Hackett had taken the receiver off its cradle so that they would assume his telephone was out of order. He had realised that that presented another danger, for if they could not communicate with Harry over the telephone, as they had done daily, they might get jittery and decide to visit the flat. But that was a chance he had to take. He had moved Harry's body to the bedroom and, after covering the bloodstained carpet with a rug, had gone out to collect the money from the bank. But now the situation had changed. With Harry lying dead in the flat he must not be there when the men came to collect the money; and since he had to get out and disappear if he wanted to remain free and in one piece he had decided he might as well take the money with him. There was a slim, a very slim chance that to leave it behind for the men to collect might get them off his back, but the discovery of Harry's body would make him the focus of a murder investigation by the police. And fifty grand could make disappearance easier, both to achieve and to endure. 'But how would Cathie be affected?' Hackett said. 'That was what I had to consider. It took me quite a while to realise that, with Harry dead, I didn't have to worry on that score. Daniel and Bernard aren't vicious, they wouldn't harm her out of spite or just for the hell of it. With me and the money gone they would almost certainly release her. After all, what else could they do?'

Hackett paused to sip whisky. 'And

then you two jokers came up with the discovery that she was being held at the farm. That put me in a right fix. There was no way I could do as you expected and call in the police, and if I didn't it would look so damned odd you might decide to consult them yourselves. That was why I had to invent my friend the Chief Constable.'

'Actually, it was the Assistant Chief Constable,' Peter said.

'Was it? No matter. You bought it.'

'Only until we went down to the farm and found that nothing was happening.'

'Oh?' Hackett held out his mug to Cathie for a refill. 'A wasted journey, eh? I was off down to the *Skye Terrier*.'

'I know. Cathie told us. She also told us — '

'Cathie told you what we decided it would be best to tell you,' Hackett interrupted. 'We wanted to condition you into identifying Harry's body as mine. If you swallowed what she told you you'd *expect* it to be mine.'

'She approved, did she?'

'Not of Harry's murder, no. But it was

an accomplished fact, and Cathie's practical. She didn't like it, but she accepted it.'

'And Lucy?' Peter asked. 'Did you accept that too, Cathie?'

'I didn't know about it,' Cathie said. 'Not till this afternoon, when Ben told me. At the time I thought . . . ' She shook her blonde head. 'No, I don't accept it. Ben was wrong, he should have found some other way. But he's my husband and I love him and — well, no matter what he's done I'm not running out on him.'

'Nor on the money either, eh?'

Cathie did not answer, but the look on her face made Peter regret the jibe. Hackett had a sudden burst of coughing and appeared not to have heard it. 'Sorry about that,' he said, the coughing over.

'Did you ask us to take the suitcase over to Guildford to get us out of the way?' Peter asked. 'Or was it to let Cathie do her conditioning bit?'

'Both,' Hackett said. 'If you'd been around you might have raised the alarm before the fire could do its job. And in addition to being conditioned we wanted you to bring Cathie back to the flat. She could have taken a taxi, of course, but her distress on arrival would have had less impact.'

Peter nodded. 'And your anxiety when Ben didn't ring was all part of the act. Eh, Cathie?'

'Yes,' she said curtly, the jibe still rankling.

'I wasn't supposed to ring,' Hackett said. 'I had this room booked, and she had the telephone number.' He smiled and looked at Cathie. 'I told you she was forgetful, didn't I? Well, she is. That's why I wrote it down for her. Not the address; just the number. Did you notice the suit I was wearing this afternoon?'

'I noticed,' Peter said. 'Ghastly!'

'That's why I chose it. For Harry. If it wasn't completely destroyed by the fire I reckoned you'd be bound to recognise it and identify the body as mine. And then there were the keys.'

'Keys?'

'To the Rover. They had to be found on the body, which meant I couldn't take the car. It would have destroyed the illusion.'

'And Harry's little finger?' Out of the corner of an eye Peter saw Cathie wince. 'When did you chop that off?'

'After I'd changed his clothes. And that wasn't easy. The limbs had stiffened, I had to break — '

'Please!' Cathie said.

'Sorry. Well, anyway, the finger had to come off. I put Harry's clothes and some of my stuff in the boot of the Rover, locked it, and then rang Daniel Fillol to tell him — '

'I know what you told him,' Peter interrupted. 'I've seen him. But why bother to ring him if you were taking the money? What was the point?'

'If you know what I told him you shouldn't have to ask,' Hackett said. 'If it were repeated to the police it would add colour to the belief that Harry had killed me. Anyway, I doused the body with paraffin, lit a fuse that would enable me to get well clear of the neighbourhood before it went up — I know about fuses, I used to work in a fireworks factory — and left. And as I came down the stairs there

276

was Lucy. In the hall.' Hackett shook his head. 'I still don't understand how she came to be there.'

Peter was puzzled by the change in the man. Presumably Hackett had been brought up in the same class of society as his cousin Daniel. Living with Cathie, however, and mixing with other well-educated people, as the money would have enabled him to do, he had no doubt schooled himself, consciously or unconsciously, to talk and behave as they did. With Cathie in the hands of his enemies and Harry constantly at his elbow he had lost some of that veneer. Now it was back; he still had his faint Cockney accent, but if there had been errors in diction or grammar Peter had not noticed them. Did that imply he was no longer under stress? Certainly he seemed relaxed and at ease. But why? Surely the stress now was as severe as in the past few days, albeit from a different cause. Or was he confident that Peter's presence presented no threat to his continued freedom?

The thought made Peter uneasy. But he explained about Lucy, although he had no explanation for why she had been in the hall. 'That certainly sounds like Lucy,' Hackett said, when he had finished.

His first thought on seeing her, he said, was that this was the end of the road. She would report — to the police, to Fillol, it didn't matter who — that he hadn't died in the fire, and the hunt would be on. And that was probably how it would have been had she not started to upbraid and threaten him. He had told her to be quiet; but she had taken no notice, and in desperation he had grabbed her and put a hand over her mouth and the other round her throat. 'I guess I panicked,' Hackett said. 'I mean, like with Harry, it wasn't a positive thing, I didn't mean to throttle her. I just wanted to silence her, to be able to think. I couldn't believe it when she went limp on me and I let her go and discovered she was dead.'

Peter felt slightly sick. Hackett had spoken quietly, but his voice had been controlled. How could a man describe the murder of his wife so calmly?

'But she was your wife!' He no longer cared whether or not Cathie was aware of that fact. 'How could you do it, man? How could you?'

'I told you, I panicked. I didn't realise what I was doing. Afterwards I was horrified. I still am when I think about it. And I suppose it was panic — the survival instinct, if you like — that made me take her body upstairs and leave it to be burnt with Harry's. I needed to destroy the physical evidence of what I had done.'

'How did you get into the flat? Wasn't the key in Harry's pocket?'

'No. I'd left it outside, as I told Daniel I would. But I had to hurry. The fuse was getting too short for comfort.'

Peter's glass was empty, but when Cathie showed him the bottle he shook his head. It flashed through his mind that they were hoping to get him drunk, in the belief that he might then be easier to handle. The whiskies had been generous. But then so had Hackett's.

'When you left Lucy after that Dyke Lane business, did you tell her where you were going?' he asked. 'Or did you just walk out on her?'

'Walked out, more or less. I told her I'd

279

let her know later where to join me, but I knew I wouldn't. We just didn't get on. She was too damned bossy. It was like being married to an R.S.M. I'd have left her anyway.'

Lucy was certainly bossy, Peter reflected. 'Is the money in there?' he asked, pointing to a suitcase.

'Most of it. Fifty grand, give or take a few hundred. I brought it with me when I left the flat. There was another ten grand in the boot of the Rover. Cathie brought that over this afternoon.'

'And that's your lot, is it?'

'In cash, yes. I own a few bits of property. But sixty grand should do us nicely for a time.'

'What time? I mean, you must have realised that even if Harry's body were identified as yours the mistake would soon be rectified. Then where would you be?'

'Lost,' Hackett said. 'With Cathie. This wasn't all planned yesterday, you know. I've always been aware that the past might catch up with me. All we needed was a couple of days' grace.'

'And now?'

'Ah!' Hackett picked up the gun and weighed it in the palm of his hand as if considering its worth. 'I don't want to use this. Certainly not in front of Cathie. I could ask her to leave, of course, but I know she wouldn't. Eh, Cathie?'

She shook her head. 'No more killing, Ben. Please!'

'No. So what's left? How are your morals, Peter? Are you susceptible to bribery?'

'I wouldn't know,' Peter said. 'I've never been exposed to it.'

'There's a biscuit tin under the dressing-table. See it?' Peter looked and nodded. 'It contains ten grand in used notes. I always kept it handy against the need for a quick get-away. Not in the flat, of course. Buried in the garden.'

'So?'

'Clear off now and forget you've been here, and you can take it with you. All of it. Ten thousand pounds.'

And that, Peter thought, explained Hackett's confidence. Bribery. And he was tempted. Conscience told him to resist the temptation, but it was there. What couldn't he do with that sort of money? And why not? It was chance that had brought him to the hotel. If Cathie hadn't forgotten her vanity case, if she hadn't dropped that slip of paper, if Dorothy hadn't seen it, if he hadn't had time to kill before meeting Andrew, he wouldn't be there, he would still believe Hackett had died in the fire. He had already identified the body as his. Why shouldn't he leave it that way and be ten thousand pounds the richer?

Hackett noticed his hesitation. 'Ever seen ten thousand quid in ready cash?' he asked. Peter shook his head. 'Well, now's your chance. Open the tin and take a look. It's a pretty sight.'

Peter placed the tin on the bed nearest to him. The lid was tight and he had difficulty in removing it. When at last it was off he looked across at Hackett.

'I don't call that pretty,' he said.

'Why not? Got greedy, have you?'

Peter lifted the tin and shook out the contents. There were no notes. Just fold upon fold of newspaper.

'What the hell?' Goggle-eyed, Hackett stood up and gaped at the mass of paper. 'Who — Christ Almighty! The bloody dustmen!'

'What dustmen?'

Almost incoherent with rage, Hackett explained. After Peter and Andrew had left the house the previous morning he had decided to recover the tin from the garden before keeping his appointment at the bank, and he had uncovered it and was lifting it from the hole when the dustmen appeared. He had put it back and waited for them to leave. 'But the damned fools didn't leave,' Hackett said. 'They squatted down and proceeded to have their elevenses. Told me the gentleman with the beard had said it would be okay and had I any objection?'

Peter nodded. 'That's true. Andrew told me he'd given them permission. He had a thing about dustmen; I believe he even supplied them with beer occasionally. Did you object?'

'How could I? I left them to it and went off to the bank. I didn't want to be late for my appointment.' Hackett swore. 'The bastards must have lifted the money while I was away.'

'But why? Even if they had noticed the tin they couldn't have known what was in it.'

'Tins like that don't get buried for no reason,' Hackett said. 'They got curious and decided to investigate.'

'But why would they bother to replace the money with newspaper? Come to that, why didn't they simply take the tin?'

'How would I know? Maybe they thought that if it looked and felt right — which it did — I wouldn't bother to check. And I didn't. Which was why I didn't chase after them. And newspapers are plentiful on a dustcart.'

'All right,' Peter said. 'So you're ten thousand light. So what do you use for a bribe?' He nodded at the suitcase. 'That?'

There came the sound of a key in the lock. Alarmed, Hackett swung round. Before he could move the door had opened and the room seemed crowded with policemen. Cathie saw guns in the hands of two of them and gave a small cry of fear. Perhaps Hackett saw them too;

bending to reach for his automatic he stopped and straightened and stood immobile, staring at the newcomers.

Superintendent Greenhough produced a handkerchief and lifted the gun from the bed.

'Sensible,' he said. 'Very sensible.'

16

Peter sat in the interview room at the police station and waited for Superintendent Greenhough. Already he was an hour late for his meeting with Andrew. He had telephoned the bar where Andrew was waiting and had given him the Kendricks' address and had told him to get over there and explain. Explain what? Andrew had asked. Explain that I'm helping the police in their inquiries and that I haven't the foggiest notion when I'll be free. That'll go down well, Andrew said, they'll probably throw me out. Get my deposit back if they do, Peter said. And had rung off.

The superintendent had left him with the assurance that he would be back in a trice. Later someone had brought him a cup of tea. That had been nearly half an hour ago. He wondered how long a trice could be in police jargon.

It turned out to be close on fifty

minutes. 'Sorry about that,' the superintendent said. He pulled a chair out from under the table and sat facing Peter. 'Something came up. Cigarette?'

'I'm trying to give them up,' Peter said.

'Sensible. Wish I could.' He flicked a lighter that sparked but refused to flame. With a muttered curse he took the cigarette from his mouth and laid it and the lighter on the table. 'Out of gas. Now, where were we?'

'We weren't anywhere,' Peter said. 'We hadn't started. You haven't even told me why I'm here.'

'Ah! Well, you're here because I wanted to question you about what went on at the Ashleigh Arms. What did Hackett tell you, what were his immediate plans? But it seems you're redundant, Mr Wilde. Hackett is singing like a canary. He's giving us the lot, including his attempt to buy your silence.' He picked up the cigarette, looked at it and put it down again. 'Could you have been bought?'

'I don't know. There wasn't a firm offer.'

'Well, that's honest, anyway. Anything

you want to ask me?'

'I thought I was here to answer questions, not to ask them.'

'So you were. Now, as I've said, you're redundant. We'll want statements from you and Mr Liston, of course, but the morning will do. No need to keep you now.'

'We'll be here,' Peter said. 'How did you know Hackett was at the Ashleigh Arms?'

'Same source as you. Through the telephone number. Miss Wellings kept the piece of paper.'

'Miss Wellings? Oh, yes — Dorothy. But why did you want him? Did you know the body wasn't his?'

'It was either his or Harry Smith's,' the superintendent said. 'And Harry Smith had a record. According to C.R.O. three of his teeth had been capped. And that went for the corpse.'

'I see. What will happen to Cathie? Mrs Hackett? Will she be charged with anything?'

'Possibly.' The cigarette was back in Greenhough's hand. Held between thumb and forefinger, he turned it over and over, tapping it against the table top. 'Except that she isn't Mrs Hackett. They aren't married, not even bigamously. She's a Miss Belsham.'

'And Fillol and the Toppings. What about them?'

'Tricky. But we'll probably think of something.' He put the cigarette in his mouth and tried the lighter again, with no more success. 'Got somewhere to sleep tonight, have you?'

'I had,' Peter said. 'I just hope it's still available.'

It was available and the Kendricks made him welcome. They were also curious. So was Andrew. It was well after midnight when he and Peter went upstairs. 'I hope you don't mind, but I've pinched the bed,' Andrew said. 'Left you the camp bed. I mean, I didn't know how heavily you were involved with the Law, did I? You could have been there all night. And it's some time since you slept in a real bed, isn't it? The camp bed will seem luxurious after that sofa.'

Peter was too tired to protest.

Two days later they collected the furniture from the flat in a van owned and driven by one of Andrew's less presentable acquaintances who answered to the name of 'Chopper'. He was a big man with a bulging stomach and a squat nose and several days growth of stubble, and a ragged fringe of hair round his bald crown. 'Looks a mess, don't it?' he said, surveying the living-room. 'Ain't hardly worth shifting that lot. Want I should take it off your hands?'

'No,' Andrew said. 'We can't all afford Chippendale.'

The room was certainly a mess. Most of the water had dried out, but in Peter's opinion the numerous burns and stains that the rugs and much of the upholstery had suffered made them fit only for the junk yard. The table too was badly marked, and many of the books were ruined. But Andrew was parting with nothing; we'll take the lot, he said, and sort it out at our leisure. You never can tell what might come in useful.

While he and Chopper shifted the bulkier items Peter packed crockery and glass and kitchenware in tea chests, tied bedding and towels and curtains into bundles, and threw out what even Andrew admitted was junk. It was a mild, warm day and by the time they were through Chopper was demanding tea. Peter pointed out that they lacked both water and electricity but that beer was available and would he settle for that? Chopper said he would.

They sat on the floor with their backs against a wall, and drank. 'We mustn't forget to call in at Number 5,' Andrew said. 'Although they're certain to hold us up. I bet they're curious as hell about what went on in the Ashleigh Arms.'

'They'll have got it all from the news media,' Peter said. 'The gist of it, anyway. But I wish we hadn't forgotten the flowers.'

'So do I. We'll have to arrange for some to be delivered.'

'Flowers?' Chopper took the bottle from his lips and pointed it at the conservatory. 'Them's flowers out there, ain't they?'

'Those, Chopper, are plants,' Andrew

said. 'No blooms. But how about them, Peter? Not leaving them, are you?'

'Of course not. We'll take them in the car. Less likely to get damaged.'

They watched Chopper depart with the van, having arranged to meet him at the guest house after lunch. Back in the conservatory Peter said, 'The prickly pear's had it, I'm afraid, and that begonia doesn't look too happy. But the rest seem all right.'

'How about these?' Andrew pointed to the boxes of earth. 'Any good?'

'We may as well take them. They might come in useful. But tip out the earth.'

He was firming the soil in one of the pots when Andrew said, 'Take a look at this, Peter.'

The suppressed excitement in his voice alerted Peter to something unusual. But he was not prepared for what Andrew had to show him. Piled on the floor amid a scattering of soil were bundles of five and ten pound notes.

'Good God!'

'The other box is the same.' Andrew pointed to where he had scraped back a thin covering of soil to expose more bundles of notes. 'It's a bloody fortune.'

Peter nodded. 'Ten thousand pounds, to be exact.'

'Eh?' Recalling Peter's account of how Hackett had tried to bribe him, the sum clicked in Andrew's mind. 'Oh, I see. Not the dustmen. Lucy, eh?'

'Who else? Hackett didn't say exactly where the tin was buried, but Lucy must have seen him uncover it and wondered what he was up to. So after he and the dustmen had gone she decided to investigate.'

'Talk about pennies from Heaven!' Andrew picked up a bundle and riffled the notes. 'Poor Lucy! She digs up a fortune and then dies before she can spend it. Sad, that.'

'Very sad,' Peter agreed. 'Although it wasn't hers to spend.'

'True. I wonder why she chose to hide it here.'

Figure it out, Peter said. She would need something in which to carry the money back to the flat, and the boxes were empty and handy; after which it would seem a logical step to cover the notes with earth and put the boxes back in the conservatory. 'She had no secure place of her own in which to hide the stuff, and she would reason that with all this schemozzle over Cathie we were unlikely to start cultivating tomatoes right away. And it would only be for a few hours. She probably intended to leave that evening, while we were out.'

'I'm surprised she didn't go earlier,' Andrew said. 'She had the place to herself in the afternoon.'

'That's true. But then, to quote Daniel Fillol, Lucy was unpredictable. On the other hand, she knew Hackett was supposed to be handing over the money next morning, and if she watched him recover the tin and stow it in the Rover she would have realised he intended to welsh. Perhaps that's why she was in the hall when he left. Trying to stop him. She'd got her whack and wanted the others to have theirs.'

'Then why didn't she try to stop him when he left after lunch?'

'Ah!' Peter shook his head. 'There you have me.'

'Well, at least I know why I couldn't find the *Telegraph* that evening,' Andrew said. 'It was in the tin, along with others.'

Andrew collected the bundles of notes from the floor, shaking them free of soil and stacking them in the box. 'What do we do with this lot?' he asked. 'A box each?'

Peter shook his head. He was thinking of Lucy. Despite a rather sour expression when she wasn't smiling, basically she had been a cheerful person. Hackett had said she was bossy, as indeed she was; but perhaps the years had tempered her bossiness, for it had always seemed good-natured. What would Lucy have done with the money? he wondered. Had she dreamt dreams as she handled it, made elaborate and exciting plans?

'We turn it in,' he said. 'You know that. Except — no, wait a minute. The finder usually gets a reward, doesn't he? Say ten per cent. That's a thousand quid. Well, don't let's be greedy. What say we settle

295

for five hundred?'

'Sure,' Andrew said. 'We settle for five hundred. Do we take it now or send the police a bill?'

'We take it now. It won't be missed. No one knows exactly how much is there.'

'No one knows that any of it is there,' Andrew said, pointing to the boxes. 'Ben knows that ten thousand quid is floating around somewhere, but he thinks the dustmen have it. What's the five hundred for? Expenses?'

'Lucy. It's hers. She found it first.'

Andrew frowned. 'That sounds a bit sick.'

'It isn't. Lucy loved ceremonials, so let's see she goes out in style. Five hundred quid should provide a slap-up funeral with all the trimmings. Agreed?'

'Agreed.'

'I mean, we owe it to her,' Peter persisted, striving to justify a decision that conscience told him others might condemn as coming from the heart rather than from the head. 'So do the jokers who actually own the money. After all, where would that ten thousand be now if Lucy hadn't unearthed it?'

'That depends, doesn't it?'

'Oh? On what?'

'As I understand it, on the strength of your resistance to bribery,' Andrew said.

THE END

We do hope that you have enjoyed reading this large print book.

Did you know that all of our titles are available for purchase?

We publish a wide range of high quality large print books including:
Romances, Mysteries, Classics
General Fiction
Non Fiction and Westerns

Special interest titles available in large print are:
The Little Oxford Dictionary
Music Book, Song Book
Hymn Book, Service Book

Also available from us courtesy of Oxford University Press:
Young Readers' Dictionary
(large print edition)
Young Readers' Thesaurus
(large print edition)

For further information or a free brochure, please contact us at:
Ulverscroft Large Print Books Ltd.,
The Green, Bradgate Road, Anstey,
Leicester, LE7 7FU, England.
Tel: (00 44) **0116 236 4325**
Fax: (00 44) **0116 234 0205**